THE ____ OF
CHEROHALA

by

Joyce Hensley Boyer

An old house up for sale, rumors of a buried treasure on the property, and suspicious activities of transient squatters, add up to a nail-biting mystery, with a dash of romance for young Tava Henner.

Her love of fine art and antique furniture, paranoia-inducing ghost stories, a runaway dog on a mission, transient squatters, and a handsome young man paying attention to the beautiful young woman spells out adventure.

When an attempt is made on her life, she learns a secret that will set her future in motion. Set in beautiful eastern Tennessee, the story harkens back to memories of southern hospitality, Civil-War era architecture, magnolia scented air, family secrets, and true love.

Copyright Information Page

ISBN-13   978-1480120808
ISBN-10   1480120804

CHAPTER ONE

"Cherohala!" Tava Henner said breathlessly. Her slate blue eyes widened at the sight of her tumble down ancestral home in East Tennessee. She eased her second handed red Ford Mercury car off Ball Play Road. Such an odd name for a road, she mused, and decided it must be an early-native American name. She drove into the overgrown drive and climbed from the car. Stepping into April's late afternoon sun, she brushed back her long coppery hair, and shivered in her tan cardigan with blue jeans.

She walked apprehensively along the weedy path toward the ghostly looking antebellum mansion. A strange prickly feeling spread over her when she remembered great Aunt Kate's ominous warning over the phone, "Don't let Cherohala ruin your life. It has happened to others!"

Whatever Aunt Kate had meant, the once grand old house appeared non-threatening, Tava decided. She suddenly stumbled over a stake protruding out of the brown grass, and stared down at a "For Sale" sign. She gasped in disbelief. "Oh, no! There must be some mistake. Dad has the first option to buy this place."

The option had been left in his Uncle Jess's will. But her dad's business had become shaky with some serious revenue decline and he couldn't take time off to look the house over. Tava had volunteered, taken advantage of her college's spring break, and driven down to look the old house over for her dad.

Still undecided about a major in her second year, she was leaning toward art design or even architecture. She'd been successful in selling her art sketches, had saved some money, gotten a small scholarship for college classes, and was looking for the perfect career opportunity for an interesting career that included her artwork and sketching, her love of antiques and old houses, and would make enough money to support her last year of college or two – especially if architectural engineering was the end result. Cherohala might be the catalyst she needed. A bed-and-breakfast or a tourist museum, or even an art gallery next to the recreational lake created from the Tellico River behind the house might be possible. While the town was small, it did attract tourists seeking a place to launch their boats, go water-skiing, or to sunbath on the grassy shores.

Why was the house for sale? She groped for an answer and vented her anger by kicking the sign, which promptly fell the rest of the way into the weeds. She would call the estate attorney the first thing in the morning and ask for an explanation. She looked around for snakes in the deep weeds, and then headed toward the house.

Tava stepped gingerly in her scruffy white sneakers up the crumbling concrete steps, which led to a wide rotting plank veranda. She made her way across the veranda, and rapped on a sturdy oak front door.

"Anybody here?" she called out, her voice sounding squeaky. After a brief pause, she felt confident no one was around and tried the knob. The door creaked open into a foyer. Tava gazed in awe at the spiral staircase. A lowboy chest stood against the opposite wall. An antique, she guessed, drawing on her knowledge from a class about antique furniture in school. She could tell how rich the wood grain was even under the thick layer of dust.

She didn't believe in the hand-me-down Cherohala ghost tales she had heard at her daddy's knee now that she was grown and determinedly ventured across the threshold for a better view of the chest. She swiped her fingers across its surface and decided it was mahogany. The smell of dust tickled her nostrils, resulting in a loud sneeze. Curiously she peered around, imagining the generations of dead Henners wandering through the hallways and napping in the darkened corners. Although this was her first visit, a feeling of déjà vu swept over her. A door slammed somewhere inside and echoed through the house.

Startled, Tava twirled around, bolted out, and fleeing to the safety of her car. After a few seconds her better judgment took over. She reasoned the wind had stolen through the old house's gaping cracks and forced a door together. She glanced back for reassurance and noticed the front door was also closed. Had she yanked it together in her haste as she fled or had it swung back automatically? Puzzling, she decided to call it a day. Cherohala could wait.

To calm herself she snatched a drawing pad from the front seat of the car and hastily sketched Cherohala's drooping facade under the bare-boned oaks. She glanced at the pencil drawing, wrinkled her nose, and tossed the sketch aside. Looking out the car window, she noticed a path zigzagging through the overgrown yard. Where did it lead? She decided to take a brisk walk and find out. It would perk her up after the long fatiguing drive from her home in Richmond, Virginia. She slid out of the car, and sank her sneakers into the sandy grass.

The sound of slow lapping water caught her ear. Her curiosity piqued when she noticed a worn path leading from the yard. Did it lead to water? She paused before following the enticing trail. Her stomach groaned noisily, reminding her it was dinnertime. At the sound of a car motor she turned around and stared. A blue Toyota Avalon swung into the drive, blocking her car. A young man emerged, and glanced about. He was tall, well proportioned with neatly trimmed tawny hair. A most handsome man, and close to her age, she decided. He glanced in her direction and waved.

Tava walked warily toward him, her heart pounding. He was nattily dressed in a navy blazer, a blue striped shirt, open collar, and gray chino trousers. He wore a watch with a leather band, a class-ring with a blue stone, but no wedding band. A boyish smile crinkled around his hazel eyes in a disarming manner.

Tava forced a shy smile in return, feeling apprehensive at his presence in this out of way place.

"Hello. I'm Shane Dumar of Zackery and Yates Realtors. We're handling this property." He gestured toward Cherohala. "I drove by and saw your car. May I help you?"

"Oh!" Tava's cheeks flushed in anger when she realized he was the agent responsible for selling Cherohala. She answered in a sharp voice.

"Yes. What's the meaning of putting a 'For Sale' sign on this place? My dad hasn't given anyone permission to sell it!" Shane shifted his stance, knitting his brow. "You sure have me confused. What's your name?"

"Sorry." She slapped her hand to her forehead and told him. Next she explained about her dad's option in his uncle's will. "My dad was unable to come. I came in his place to look it over. If we decide not to buy it, then it will go on the market."

"Ah." Shane broke into a grin. "Now I understand why you're upset. I remember hearing about that will." He cocked his head. "I suppose I didn't connect it with Cherohala when my boss, Hobe Yates, asked me to put the sign out here last week."

"Cherohala has been on the market for a week!" Tava's eyebrows shot up.

"It could have been sold!"

"Not likely in that short time. Besides it's priced sky high. Sorry about the mix-up. I'll check it out with Hobe. I'm sure he'll get to the bottom of it."

"Good." Tava intended to get it cleared through the estate lawyer also. "Of course you'll remove the sign."

Shane frowned. "Would you mind if I left it for my boss to pick up? After all it was his mistake."

"That's okay with me." She realized the need to clear it with his superior. "I hear water," she said pleasantly, hoping to make amend, "Is there a river nearby?"

"Yes. The Tellico River, but now a lake." He glanced toward her car's license. "I see you're from out of state. Have you heard about the dam that backed the water over part of Cherohala's bottom land?"

"No," She shook her head, and wondered how much the water lowered the value of the property. Shane glanced at his watch. "Would you like for me to show you the house and grounds. I'm good at that sort of thing." He chuckled.

Tava assumed he was trying to make up for the snafu and started to accept his offer. On second thought she demurred.

"Thank you, but not today. It's almost dark and my aunt is expecting me soon."

"Tomorrow morning then?"

"I'd like that. What time?"

He reached into his jacket breast pocket, pulling out a small black appointment book, and business card. Handing Tava the card, he flipped open the book, and asked, "How about 10 o'clock?"

"Perfect." Tava beamed, and dropped the card into her shoulder bag; thrilled at the chance to see him again.

"I've heard Cherohala has a fascinating history," he said, as if he were trying to delay his departure.

"Does it still have a haunted reputation?" Tava giggled. "My dad used to tell me stories about it all the time, about how used to visit and get spooked by swinging doors, bumps in the night, and stuff going missing."

"Don't tell me you're a nonbeliever!" His eyes sparkled mischievously. "I bet you are still young enough to believe most of them, too!"

"Any house over a hundred years old is likely to have ghosts and secrets." Tava laughed. "I grew up on dad's Cherohala tales. And, not I'm not that young to still believe in such tales, I just turned twenty-one, thank you very much!"

Shane grinned, "Then you know about the hidden treasure, but are too old to believe it such nonsense then?"

"Hidden treasure!" Tava's eyes narrowed in disbelief. "You're kidding, of course. My dad must have forgotten that one or I've forgotten – it has been quite a few years. Tell me about it."

Shane shrugged. "There's not much to tell. Something valuable was supposedly hidden somewhere near Cherohala during the War Between the States and never found."

"Really! Any truth to the story?"

"You can't prove it to me." He held up his hands. "It does make good conversation. The man who told me that story, Rance Bottoms, lives over there." He glanced around, pointing over his shoulder.

"I met him last week. He's full of spooky tales about the old house."

Tava turned and scanned the area. All she saw was a shed-like building in the distance. Perhaps Shane meant farther down. It didn't seem important and she dismissed it. Instead she mentioned Cherohala's unlocked door.

"What!" Shane grimaced. "The door is unlocked!"

Tava nodded.

"Careless me!" He shook his head. "I was positive I locked it." He rammed his hand in his pants' pocket, took out keys on a ring, and jingled them, as he hurried toward the house. He clipped up the steps with the agility of an athlete and opened the front door. He locked it, and returned. "I can't imagine why I forgot to lock it! By the way, what's your aunt's name?'

"Kate Linley."

"I know her."

"She's my great aunt. She's the sister to dad's Uncle Jess. I'll be staying with her."

""I've never met her in person, but she seemed nice over the phone. Do you know how to get to her house? It's not far from here."

"I have directions." She opened her shoulder bag, and started rummaging for the MapQuest directions.

"You don't need written directions...I'll show you the way. She lives less than a mile from here." He indicated with a wave of his hand and strode over to Tava's car, opening the door.

"Thank you," Tava said, feeling a comfortable warmth as she slid onto her car seat. Shane closed her door gallantly and hurried to his car. After revving his motor, he backed out, and was soon speeding down the blacktop Ball Play Road.

Tava's heart thumped crazily as she followed him. The mix-up over the sale of Cherohala receded in her mind. Could she have fallen in love with this man at first sight? Impossible, she assured herself…that only happened in movies and novels! Was the attraction his irresistible personality and his special knack of putting one at ease? Perhaps that's why he chose to be a salesman. He was quite handsome and seemed very sweet on her. Up ahead Shane slowed his car and honked the horn. He motioned toward a two-story, white-framed house on a spacious lawn surrounded by giant oak trees whose limbs seemed to reach up toward the clouds.

Tava waved back. After watching him speed away, she turned into Aunt Kate's driveway. The sweet thought of Shane was broken by a nagging thought – how could she expect a charming young man like him to be available? She brushed the negative thought aside. She'd see him tomorrow morning. That was sufficient for the moment. Her pulse quickened.

CHAPTER TWO

"You're Tava!" Aunt Kate, bone thin and silver haired, exclaimed. She ushered her in the front door.

"I'd know you anywhere." Aunt Kate wore a loosely fitted pink pantsuit. She appeared as chirpy as a cricket, despite her age. She embraced Tava as if she had known her all her life and led her into a bright cheery sitting room.

"I'm glad you got here safe and sound." Aunt Kate smiled, and raised her clasped hands. "I worried about you driving 500 miles in traffic on the interstate by yourself."

"My mother worried too. I have a cell phone and I'm a pretty good driver," Tava said, and eased her luggage along the carpeted floor. Tava didn't bother telling her great-aunt she used to drive hundreds of miles for places to sketch and draw for her art. Tava gazed about wide-eyed at the whimsical decor of the room, filled with white Priscilla curtains, fanciful bric-a-brac, and light blue upholstered chairs, which reminded her of a spring garden. "What a charming room!"

Aunt Kate's face glowed. "I'm glad you like it."

A bouquet of pungent scented lavender lilacs atop a Pembroke table intermingled with the aroma of freshly baked bread. It reminded Tava she hadn't eaten since noon. Aunt Kate fluttered about and almost stumbled over a shaggy brindled dog. She gave the dog a gentle nudge with her sneaker.

"This is Pepper." Pepper wagged his tail, and sniffed with his button nose at Tava's hand. He was medium sized and appeared to be a hodge-podge breed.

"Hi, Pepper," Tava said, and reached down, stroking his head. "You look exactly like your name."

"Sometimes he gets a bit out of control. He usually growls at strangers," Aunt Kate said. "Seems he's taken a fancy to you. Maybe his obedience training has paid off."

"He senses I'm an animal lover."

Aunt Kate stared unabashedly at Tava. "I can't get over how lovely you are. There's an old saying any girl with a drop of Henner blood is bound to be pretty. You're a Henner through and through with your smile and pretty complexion. And look at that beautiful red hair!"

Tava blushed self-consciously. "Thank you."

"That old adage didn't work for me, Aunt Kate." The grating voice came from the doorway. A thickset lady, in a black paisley print dress with dark hair pulled back in a severe chignon, entered the room. She moved with a certain air of authority.

"Oh! This is Dottie Spinnet," Aunt Kate gestured. "She lives with me and works at the bank."

Dottie, hugging forty, and wearing rimless tinted glasses, waved her hand.

"Hi, Tava. I knew you were coming. Aunt Kate told the whole neighborhood. I'm your cousin. I moved in with Aunt Kate after I was widowed. She spoiled me so, I just gave up looking for a place closer to town."

She plopped down in a blue upholstered Queen Anne wing chair and crossed her legs. She glared at Tava with a deprecating grin and said, "You came all this distance to buy a tumble down and ill-fated old house!"

Tava was taken back by Dottie's obvious putdown and said, "I came to look the house over for my dad."

Dottie sounding like a cross examiner asked, "If your father buys the place, does he to intend to tear the house down?"

"Nothing has been decided yet, but I'm not in favor of tearing it down. I can visualize a restored antebellum showplace," Tava said.

"Such a pity!" Aunt Kate's voice quivered. "The old house is in such a state of disrepair and holds such rich and historic memories."

Tava stared at Aunt Kate in astonishment. "You think the house should be torn down?"

Aunt Kate nodded; a faraway look in her eyes.

"My dad has happy memories of Cherohala," Tava said.

Dottie adjusted her glasses on her nose. "Did your dad tell you about the first owner of Cherohala, Erk Henner, and the tragedies during the War Between the States?"

"No." Tava shook her head. "It seems he left out quite a bit."

"Have a seat," Dottie pointed to the sofa in an authoritative way. "Aunt Kate is good at telling the story, if you're interested."

"Sure," Tava said politely and sank down on the blue floral sofa draped in bright colored crocheted throws. Annoyed at Dottie's take-charge manner, and unable to escape, she steeled herself for the expected boring tale.

Aunt Kate, eager to begin, sat down beside Tava and folded her hands in her lap.

"This part of East Tennessee was unusual in what some folks still call 'the recent unpleasantness,'" Aunt Kate smiled. "Neighbors who had been friends all their lives became enemies overnight if they chose to pick different political sides."

Tava perked up. "I didn't know it was like that in this area. Which side was Erk Henner on?"

"He leaned toward the Union's viewpoint of keeping the states together, regardless of the consequences," Aunt Kate said. "You see in this part of the county many folks didn't want to break up the country. Erk's oldest son, Isaac, your great-great grandfather, joined the Federal Troops. The second son, David, had other ideas. He slipped away and joined the Confederacy. Erk put his foot down when it came to his third son, Horace, who was fifteen."

Tava, her interest whetted, perched on the edge of the sofa and interrupted. "I've read about brothers who fought each other in the war, but I didn't know it happened in the Henner family."

Aunt Kate nodded. "Rumors of bushwhackers and deserters in the area left everyone with many strained family relationships. One night Erk was away from home on business and a neighbor warned the family a stranger was seen lurking about. Horace, armed with a Bowie knife, decided to carry a chest of family heirlooms somewhere outside to hide in a safe place from any thieves or bushwhackers. When he didn't return, his mother and sisters went looking for him."

"Oh." Tava caught her breath, fearing the story would end tragically.

Aunt Kate lowered her voice, whispering in a dramatic undertone, "They found Horace dying in the river bottom. He'd been stabbed and was moments from dying. His knife was never found and the family's rowboat was missing. His last words were, 'Click's Bluff.' That's the largest river cliff."

Tava wiped a tear from her eye. "How sad. Did they ever find the chest?"

Aunt Kate shrugged. "No. The family searched all over and after the dam was built, everyone assumed if it were still out there, it's covered with hundreds of feet of water now."

"There really is a hidden treasure!" Tava gulped. "Shane Dumar indicated something like that to me, but I thought he was teasing! Did they ever find Horace's killer?"

"Probably." Aunt Kate continued. "They figured the killer escaped in the family's rowboat. A few days later some stranger's body was fished downstream from the Tellico River. A Bowie knife was tucked in his belt that looked like Erk's, but the boat was long gone. But no real proof was ever conclusive – who knows, the dead man may have been killed by Erk's killer, too."

"What happened to Isaac and David after the war?" Tava asked.

Aunt Kate cleared her throat. "David returned in a pine box. He was killed in a battle near Chattanooga, but they didn't bury him in the family cemetery because of the shame of going to the Confederacy's side. There were rumors Isaac actually fought in the same battle in which his brother died. Isaac came home and wouldn't talk to anyone about the war, had to care for an ailing father who died soon after the war ended, and a grieving mother who was close to going insane with the loss of her boys."

"Erk died of grief, no doubt," Dottie added. "Two son's dying because of the war, and the embarrassment of one son fighting against his brother probably broke his heart."

"How tragic!" Tava said.

"It's true the war was the source of many of the Henner family tragedies," Dottie said. "But the bad luck continued after the War. Many of the Henners who lived at Cherohala were plagued with calamities. Isn't that right, Aunt Kate?"

Aunt Kate nodded, her face somber. "Isaac's youngest son drowned in the river, and a granddaughter died from injuries received in a fall down the spiral stairway at Cherohala. Erk's wife, Ada, wasn't all right in her mind when she passed."

"True," Dottie said, nodding vigorously.

"My brother Jess, lived there last, lost his wife in childbirth. His only son, Jess, Jr., died in early manhood, leaving two small sons," Aunt Kate said.

Tava gaped. "Now I understand why you feel Cherohala is an ill-fated house."

"Jess doesn't agree with me, of course," Aunt Kate said. "The house seemed to cast a spell over him."

"Only Henners have ever lived in the house," Dottie added. "Aunt Kate, you left out the weird part."

"You can call it weird if you want." Aunt Kate pursed her lips. "Some folks call it the Ghost of Cherohala!"

Tava grinned slyly at the absurdity. "I thought the Cherohala ghost stories were for scaring naughty children?"

"Of course, you're right," Aunt Kate's face reddened. "But there have been sights and sounds in that house that no one could explain. Not even Jess."

Tava remembered her scare from the banging door. She had convinced herself it had been the wind, and surely there were logical explanations for the sights, too. She kept these opinions to herself for now.

"Tava, where did you meet Shane?" Dottie asked.

Tava filled them in on the 'For Sale' sign at Cherohala.

"That's news to me!" Dottie said. "Had you heard it, Aunt Kate?"

Aunt Kate looked up. "No."

"I'm surprised I didn't hear about it in this small town," Dottie cocked, her head in thought. "I know both John Zackery and Hobe Yates, the realty partners. I can't imagine them making a mistake like that! Are you sure your dad's option hasn't expired?"

"I hope not!" Tava clapped her hand to her mouth. A chill spread over her. Could her dad have been that careless? She recalled the news of his good fortune, and had been overjoyed at the idea of restoring an old mansion. Her dad didn't appear excited, citing financial problems in his advertising agency. After much persuasion, he gave her permission to check on the property.

"I'll call the attorney and see about the option the first thing in the morning."

Dottie asked, "Did Shane flirt with you some, Tava?"

"Uh..." Tava's face blushed at the personal question. "Yes, I suppose he did. He seemed helpful and well mannered."

"That describes Shane," Aunt Kate chimed in. "He's handsome too. I reckon I've known him for a long time. Ever since his folks moved back here."

"Handsome is as handsome does, I've always heard." Dottie clucked her tongue.

"Oh?" Tava's eyebrows shot up. "What do you mean?"

"Shane can be charming or stand-offish, according to his mood." Dottie pushed her glasses upon her nose. "He's a mighty popular bachelor at twenty-five. If you're interested in him, you may have to take a number and stand in line."

"I...I just met him," Tava mumbled, and felt a bit disconcerted.

"I've heard he's quite picky about his girl friends." Dottie nodded confidentially. "He's broken one engagement."

"Really?" Tava felt uncomfortable over the turn of the conversation. She gave a weary shrug, and stood up. "Aunt Kate, could you show me my room?"

"Of course." Aunt Kate arose. "It's upstairs. After you put your things away, come down and eat. I'll warm your supper in the microwave."

Tava picked up her bag and followed Aunt Kate up the carpeted stairs with Pepper at their heels.

They were half way up the stairs when Dottie's voice rang out. She stood at the bottom of the stairway. "Tava, you'll have to forget about Shane. Aunt Kate and I weren't thinking straight. He's your cousin."

Tava paused, responding with an absent stare over her shoulder at the unwelcome revelation. Now she understood why the proverbial bearers of bad news were often killed.

She continued up the stairway. Her bag turned lead-like and her knees mimicked jelly. She trailed Aunt Kate into an ultra-feminine bedroom; wallpapered in miniature, pink rosebuds. She plunked her luggage down between a mahogany pencil post bed and a blue velvet boudoir chair.

She sighed with an air of resignation. Her desire for a romance with Shane dashed and the future of Cherohala uncertain.

Aunt Kate directed Tava to a closet for her clothes and said, "It's nice to have a young person around for a change."

"Thank you." Tava forced a smile. "It's sweet of you to take me in on such a short notice."

"I'm glad you came, dear. I hope I didn't discourage you by those scary tales."

"I don't give up easily," Tava said, hoping her trip hadn't been in vain. Aunt Kate pointed to the bathroom across the hall and shooed Pepper out of the room. She turned to go, but hung back at the door. She spoke in a low voice, her brown eyes twinkling. "Shane's what we call a distant, kissing cousin."

"Really?" Tava grinned; her spirits lifted, beginning to develop a liking for this spritely, spirited old woman. "You're all right, Aunt Kate."

She patted Aunt Kate's arm, knowing she had found a friend.

CHAPTER THREE

Tava raced along in her car to Cherohala. She was jubilant over the news from the attorney. Her dad's option to buy the place was still open. The Realtors had made the mistake. She parked in the drive near a silver BMW promptly at 10 o'clock. Eager with anticipation at seeing Shane again, she gaped at the elegant automobile. She hopped out of her car, dressed in a blue pastel sweater over a teal blue calico skirt, and slammed the door. The morning air felt crisp around the edges and thickening clouds scudded across the sky.

Expecting to see Shane alight from the BMW, Tava looked up with a start. A mature, heavy-set man with dark eyes and dark hair slid out. He greeted her, and his face lighted up with a smile. He was dressed casually, yet impeccable in a cream cashmere sweater over a tan shirt. He wore a yellow polka dot tie with beige slacks. His diamond solitaire ring and Rolex watch impressed her with the scent of money. He yanked nervously at his tie, and extended his hand, emitting a pleasant woodsy smell of after-shave lotion.

"I'm Hobe Yates, junior partner of Zackery and Yates Realtors. You're Tava, of course."

"Good morning, Mr. Yates." Tava responded with an outstretched hand. His hand was warm and moist, his handshake firm.

"Call me Hobe. Everybody does."

Wonder where was Shane is, Tava puzzled, screwing up her face with this setback.

"You're wondering what happened to Shane," Hobe said, as if Tava's thoughts were transparent.

"All the young and pretty girls ask for him." He grinned, and waved a hand. "I came in his place to apologize for my mistake. I misread the date when the option expired. You see, we were asked to sell Cherohala if your father didn't want it. I suppose you called your lawyer, and got it straightened out."

"Yes." Tava said. "I talked to an attorney by the name of Elisa Rhodes."

"Oh, yes. The lovely Elisa," Hobe nodded gleefully. "Shane is with her this morning. She's new in town and a prima donna...seems to have hit it off with Shane."

Tava experienced a surge of jealousy at the mention of Shane and the new attorney in town. She averted her eyes to conceal the disappointment, although she'd only met him yesterday, and had no right to feel like the way she did. Immediately she chided herself. She reminded herself that the sole purpose of her visit was to evaluate the condition of the old mansion, Cherohala, and advise her dad accordingly. Thoughts of involvement were out of the question. She would return to her home and college. Any romantic feelings must be banished from her mind.

"Are you ready for the tour?" Hobe asked.

"Yes." Tava nodded, and felt something brush against her leg. Startled, she glanced down. Pepper circled her feet. "Pepper! You followed me!"

"You brought your dog along?'

"No. He followed me. He's Aunt Kate's dog. He seems to have become attached."

"Smart dog." Hobe guffawed. He bent over with an outstretched hand and patted Pepper.

Pepper growled, and eyed Hobe warily. Hobe drew back. "He's not very friendly!"

"Pepper! Stop growling and go home." Tava ordered.

Pepper backed off, staring up at Tava with doleful eyes. After the second scolding, he tucked his tail between his legs, and slunk away.

"Pepper should be nicer. Aunt Kate has taken him to obedience school."

Hobe shrugged. "What would you like to see first, the property lines or the old house?"

"The property lines," she said, thinking she'd leave the best until last.

She needed to inspect the house and furnishings meticulously.

"The Ball Play Road, the one you came in on, and the lake waters are two of the place's boundaries." Hobe waved his hand. "There are markers for the other ones. Let's walk down to the lake and circle back."

Hobe led the way following a footpath, which zigzagged through the yard and skirted an apple orchard. Swarms of bees buzzed around pinkish-tinted apple blossoms. Chirping sparrows winged in and out of the thickening foliage. The trail continued through a cluster of overgrown vines. Briary branches reached out like clawing fingers. Shortly they were at the water's edge.

Tava sucked in her breath. "It's beautiful! I'm surprised it hasn't become some sort of a fishing resort!"

"Yes," Hobe agreed. "It's the back water from the Tellico River dam and it does have possibilities. One would need more capital than it's worth to develop such an undertaking." The rustic scene would be perfect for sketching, Tava thought, reveling in its beauty. Farther along tall chalky cliffs arose ghostly pale upon the horizon. Nearby, a battered rowboat anchored to a willow tree at the water's edge bobbed and bumped with the flow. It reminded Tava of Aunt Kate's Civil War story.

"Whose boat?" Tava asked, imagining it was similar to the one Horace Henner's killer escaped in.

"Probably some old fisherman who likes to fish in different spots,"

Hobe said. "This was once a large river farm. Your ancestors sold off land through the years. I believe Jess Henner had about fifty acres before the dam was built. There's considerable less now."

Tava, with scant knowledge of open spaces, was impressed with the remaining tract. "It's hard for me to imagine owning this much land."

"No big deal in this rural area."

They trekked along the boundary lines. Near the road they passed a once red barn in need of repair. Rusting farm implements were strewn about. A shed-like building with a window on one side, and a chimney pipe sprouting from the roof stood near the barn.

Tava pointed to the shed. "I noticed that building yesterday. But I didn't see the chimney pipe or the window. What's it used for?"

"Rance Bottoms, the late Jess Henner's handyman lives there." He explained.

"Shane mentioned Rance yesterday," Tava said. "I didn't realize he lived on the property. What will happen to him if the property is sold?"

"I don't know." Hobe shrugged. "I'm sure he'll find another home."

Tava blinked. Did she sense a lack of compassion in Hobe? Then again he had no control of the matter. If her dad bought the place, it would become their concern. She decided to worry about that later. The clouds darkened, and the breeze sped up, blowing Tava's hair about her face. "It looks like rain," she said.

"I think we'd better hurry back to the house," Hobe said, quickening his pace. "Too bad your dad couldn't come and look over the place."

"Dad's familiar with all this." Tava waved her hand, as she hurried along. "Growing up, he spent many summers here with Uncle Jess."

"He wouldn't recognize the place now. The tumbledown house, the bottomlands flooded with water, the land wild and overgrown. What does he plan to do with it, if he buys it?" Hobe asked.

Tava hesitated, feeling uncomfortable over the question. The discussion about the land and the house with her dad had been mostly one sided, hers, and centered around restoring the old mansion.

"It will probably depend on several things," she hedged. "Would it make a good investment?"

"Well…" He wrinkled his nose. "What can I say? I suppose all land is a good investment to someone who needs it. I don't know why Jess didn't give your dad the place outright. The option price is ridiculously low. Your dad would never move here, would he?"

"No." Tava shook her head. "I don't know what he'd want with it then," Hobe said. "If he decides to buy it, I'll take it off his hands any time at a generous profit. I'm serious. Have him call me."

"What would you do with Cherohala?" Tava asked.

"I'm a realtor. That's what we do, buy and sell. Mostly we sell for our clients. Occasionally an owner needs to sell quickly, and there are no takers. Then we buy the property. Down the road, the right person will come along."

A chill inched down the nape of Tava's neck at the idea of giving up the ancestral home, despite its run-down condition and ill-fated reputation. She feared Hobe's offer might be exactly what her dad was looking for: quick cash for his ailing business. She furrowed her brow. "I'll tell my dad about your offer."

"I don't mean to sound pushy, but your dad needs to make up his mind quickly. I suppose you know his option runs out in a week."

Tava stopped in her tracks, and caught her breath. "I know!"

Hobe shrugged. "He's had three months to make up his mind."

Tava took a quick step to catch up, reasoning her dad had neglected to tell her the date his option ran out because of his pressing business distractions. Could she convince him to buy

Cherohala in one short week? It was sufficient time for her to decide, but her mind was already made up the first time she saw it. It might be too soon for her dad to decide because of his failing business.

Dark clouds gathered and churned. A thunderclap peeled across the heavens, fat raindrops pounded on Tava's head. She and Hobe began to run and raced the last few yards to the old house, dashing onto the long ell-shaped back porch. Rusting strips of mesh from the once screened enclosure swayed from the porch posts. Tava, wet and bedraggled, blotted her face and hair with tissues from her shoulder bag. Hobe mopped his face and hair with a white, richly monogrammed handkerchief.

When Tava regained her composure, she stared at the backside of the deteriorating old house. Looking beyond its lack of maintenance—peeling paint, falling chimneys, and missing shutters—she envisioned a lovely renovated Southern home. "I believe this house could be restored," she blurted.

"You too!" Hobe frowned. "You'll change your mind when you see the inside."

"It's that bad!"

"Believe me. It would take more time and money than it's worth." Hobe yanked at his tie. "You remind me of Dottie Spinnet. You know her?"

"I met her last night." Tava said. "She's a cousin who lives with my Aunt Kate."

"She's a character!" Hobe grinned. "And a pal of mine." He fumbled in his pocket, and pulled out a key ring. "She thinks this old tumble down house can be restored too." "

"She does?" Tava puzzled, crinkling her nose. She had gotten the wrong impression of Dottie.

"I have a suggestion." Hobe rattled his keys. "Let me take you to lunch. There's a unique little café in town. It's called the Lunch Box, and specializes in noon meals. You know, soups, salads and sandwiches. After we eat we can come back and go through the house as leisurely as you like." He licked his lips. "I'm starved, aren't you?"

"Hmm." Tava hesitated. "I'm sorry, but I'm not in the least bit hungry. Aunt Kate went all out this morning, and served a huge breakfast; bacon, eggs, biscuits and apple jelly. I'm afraid I pigged out." She glanced at Hobe's seemingly dejected face, and quickly added, "It sounds like a delightful place. Could I have a rain check?"

"Sure." He nodded. "We don't have to eat now. I'll stay and show you through the house. I can stand a few hunger pains." He patted his trim middle.

Tava glanced at the time on her watch. "No. You go on. It's lunchtime. Thanks for offering to stay with me. But I really need to poke about, and examine everything carefully. You'd be miserable."

"But you'll be alone!" He raised his hand. "Aren't you afraid?"

"Uh…" Tava hitched up her shoulders. "I suppose I'll be all right. As long as the doors don't slam."

"What do you mean?" he asked.

Tava grinned sheepishly, and told him of her scare the day before.

A slow grin broke across his face. "Ah. You heard the Ghost of Cherohala!" He reared back and laughed.

Slightly irritated, Tava's face reddened.

I'm sorry," he said, as if he hadn't meant to offend. "Of course, you don't believe in ghosts."

"Not since I was a child."

"Then you'll be fine." He handed her the house keys. "You might as well keep them. I won't need them, unless…well, you know." He shrugged. "I'd advise you to lock the door when you get inside."

"Really? Why?"

"Just in case." He waved his hand. "You'll be alone in an old empty house in an isolated area."

Tava decided the thought was a bit unsettling, and patted her shoulder bag. "I brought my cell phone."

"Good. Don't forget the rain check lunch date." He winked.

"I won't." She forced a smile. Asking for a rain check seemed the polite thing to do. Although Hobe appeared courteous and sophisticated, he seemed a bit old and he wasn't her type. She waved to him as he darted into the rainstorm toward his car.

A bit hesitant she inserted the key into the back door lock, and twisted the doorknob. With a scraping sound the door slowly opened. Tava entered the kitchen of the old house, full of hope.

CHAPTER FOUR

Tava entered the kitchen in the old house, and relocked the door. She gazed open mouthed at the large room with a high ceiling, and blackened walls. A stale odor hung in the air. Gray rainy light seeped though the narrow and yellowed windows scalloped in cobwebs and she shivered in the dampness.

She crept cautiously about, as if she were muffling the sound of her presence. A kitchen floor plank creaked under the worn and discolored linoleum at each step. She winced. Her arms broke out in goose bumps. She wished she hadn't been so adamant that Hobe leave! She had to jack up her courage, and do what she came to do – look around the house – and examine everything carefully.

A black iron stove with four burner eyes, a warming closet at the top, and a water tank on the side backed up against a closed up fireplace. She chuckled at the multi-purpose use of the wood-burning cook stove. The woodbin must have been nearby. What a chore to chop wood, and keep enough on hand to cook a meal! Another use for the stove would have been to heat the room and surrounding area in cold weather. Tava sighed a thankful note for the amenities of today. Across the room sat a long kitchen table covered with a faded and wrinkled oilcloth. Dusty modern kitchen appliances were placed at the other end of the room for use. It was an odd blending of the old with the new. Tava visualized a dab of paint here, a snippet of wallpaper there, and sunny patterned cottage curtains for the windows. Voila – a charming country kitchen!

Her grandiose ideas were interrupted by a scratching noise. Forgetting her plans, she stood stone still, and listened intently. The sound came from the direction of the back door. When the scratching evolved into a whine, she recognized it at once, and giggled at her fear. She hurried to the door, unlocked it, and peeked through. Pepper gazed up at her in his amber woe-be-gone eyes.

"Pepper! I told you to go home," she scolded, hunkering down, and rubbing his rain-soaked muzzle. "Sorry, Pepper, I can't let you come in. You're dripping wet, and it's not my house yet. Go home now." She pushed him away with her hand, and closed the door.

Tava sauntered back through the kitchen, and into the dining room, chuckling over Pepper's attachment to her. A wooden pie cupboard, with tin doors, stood near another fireplace. The cupboard was dwarfed by the emptiness of the large dining room. In the right front parlor, wainscoted in oak. Tava examined an antique organ with a mirrored top. She strummed her fingers across the ivory keys. Several keys sounded dead and made a cacophony of noises. A decrepit and dusty tan couch sat across from the fireplace. The left parlor contained a fireplace, an old fashioned oaken desk, and two broken down armchairs.

Tava remembered the lowboy in the foyer from yesterday and hurried through the hallway to look it over again. She stared dumbfounded at the empty space. What had happened to the beautiful antique lowboy? Had she imagined it? Or had she seen it elsewhere and confused the place? Surely her mind wasn't playing tricks on her! She shrugged it off and re-entered the hallway. Leaning against the handrail of the stairway, she peered up the stairs and wondered if there were antiques on the second floor. She hesitated before she took the first step up the stairs. An uneasy feeling gripped her, making her pause. Had the old house and the rainstorm triggered her edginess? This was something she had to do. She couldn't let her fear hold her back. Steeling herself, she crept up the stairs.

More rainy light filtered through a window at the top of the landing. Tava became calmer, and counted the closed doors on both sides of the hallway. She eased open the first door on the right, and peered inside. It was another room with a fireplace. One in every room, she assumed. A nightstand in walnut finish stood near a dark bedstead with a headboard reaching halfway to the ceiling. Unglued wallpaper dangled from a corner in the room.

The next room was bare. Tava continued to the end room. It contained a single piece of furniture – a bulky mahogany looking armoire with a broken pediment top. Intrigued by the wardrobe, Tava walked over, and opened both doors. There were cotton flannel blankets and patchwork quilts stacked on one side, with a faint odor of mothballs clinging to them. Two dark woolen and worn men's suits hung on the other side. She pinched her nose to suppress a sneeze.

Tava decided the suits had belonged to Uncle Jess. She made a mental measure of him by the size of the suits. He definitely seemed to have been a tall man. She closed the armoire doors and viewed the room with two windows. It would make a lovely study with an easy chair by the fireplace and a desk by the window overlooking the driveway. She glanced out, and saw her car parked in the driveway.

When a banging noise echoed from below, she caught her breath with a start. It shattered her reverie. A door slammed again – this time it was much louder. Tava had not noticed a wind outside in the rain. She had no intention of running, because there was no place to go without running into the intruder, who no doubt had slammed the door! Was it an inside or back door? Had she forgotten to lock the door after she closed it to Pepper? Perhaps it wasn't an intruder after all, if a gust of wind had blown it open. Pepper could have wandered in. She felt better at the thought. Tava had seen nothing in the house so far, that Pepper could possibly damage. She decided to go down, and check. Over the incessant din of raindrops on the roof, heavy footsteps sounded from below. Halfway across the room, Tava froze in her tracks. There had to be a person downstairs. Perhaps Hobe had changed his mind and returned. She glanced out both windows. All she saw was her blue Chevy.

Her heart raced. She didn't see Hobe's car or any other one. Who could it be? The name Rance Bottoms came to mind.

"Who's there?" she yelled, her voice reverberating. She waited with bated breath for an answer. In the silence, numbness inched over her body. What kind of man would wander into an old house, knowing someone was inside, and not announce his presence? She clapped her hand to her mouth. She knew the answer.

When the footsteps pounded on the stairs, Tava stood terror-stricken.

Was he coming for her? He had heard her yell and knew she was upstairs. Her thoughts raced wildly. Her only hope was he didn't know which room. Where could she hide? She swung around facing the armoire. That was it. She raced to it, clawed it open, and scrambled inside. She closed the doors, and crouched down between the quilts and woolen suits. She fervently hoped a sneeze wouldn't betray her.

When Tava heard the intruder tramping up the stairs and the hallway outside the room, she curled into a ball, praying he didn't enter. Heavy footsteps sounded inside the room. Tava's heart battered against her breast so loudly, she feared he would hear it. She barely breathed, squeezed her phone, and readied herself to dial for help. She expected to be found momentarily. It seemed an eternity of seconds ticked by before the footsteps left the room and faded down the stairs. Tava breathed a sigh of thankfulness, but remained in the armoire in case he returned. Not even a phone call could have saved her quick enough.

She waited ample time for the trespasser to leave. When all seemed quiet, she emerged, tingling all over from the fear and cramped position. She breathed deeply, stretched, and wobbled toward the window over the driveway. She saw no one.

Still trembling, she sneaked down the stairs, half expecting to bump into him at any moment. She checked the back door, which was locked. She hurried through the house and examined the front door. It was locked also. The intruder had a key!

She ventured outside cautiously and peered around for some sign of the culprit. She saw no one. The rain shower had ended and the clouds had broken up. Shafts of sunlight shone through the trees, filling the bare branches with glints of silver. Tava waded through the moisture-laden grass, soaking her sneakers. Her enthusiasm for browsing through Cherohala had evaporated.

Pepper darted out from an azalea bush, shook himself, splattered Tava, and trotted along beside her.

"Pepper, you don't obey very well." She stopped short at her car, and puzzled. "Pepper, why didn't you bark at the man who scared me half to death?"

Pepper wagged his tail.

The question bothered Tava. She knew Pepper's habit for barking at strangers. She stroked his head.

She felt braver with Pepper at her side and glanced back at the old house and remembered Hobe's remark about Cherohala's ghost. That was no ghost that searched for her. The footsteps were loud and clear.

CHAPTER FIVE

Anger flashed over Tava at the traumatic experience in the old house. How dare an intruder ruin her day! She turned on her heels; her courage puffed up in the bright sunshine. She folded her arms and vowed to re-enter Cherohala. She'd check each room and every stick of furniture in detail. She stared at the house before retracing her steps. Her common sense intervened and she reluctantly called it a day. She would return to Aunt Kate's. She opened the car door, glancing about. She sucked in her breath at what she saw. Her left front tire was flat.

"Drats!" she said, stepping back, and taking stock of the situation. The tire was practically new. Could she have picked up a nail in the driveway? Nonchalantly, she opened the car trunk, and took out a tire iron, jack, and spare. She worked furiously, thankful she knew how it was done, sweating in the damp heat left by the thunderstorm, toiling until the wheel was off and the spare was on.

A trip into town would be necessary. No need to risk another flat without a spare. The changing of the tire, the humidity filled air, and the warm rays of the sunshine made her feel uncomfortable. She nudged up her sweater sleeves and wiped the perspiration from her forehead with the back of her hand. Plunking the flat and the tools back inside the trunk, she rubbed her hands together to remove the loose dirt. Out of the corner of her eye, she saw Pepper turn away and wag his tail.

Wheeling around, she faced a middle-aged man with deep-set blue eyes staring at her. He wore a red checked shirt with faded blue jeans.

"Oh!" She gulped in surprise.

"Howdy, Miss. I didn't mean to startle you. I'm Rance Bottoms. I live on the place." He had a leathery face, a tight mouth, as if he never smiled. Tufts of gray hair stuck out from under a dark blue denim cap. He jerked his thumb backward. "You're the Henner girl, of course."

"Yes, I'm Tava." She nodded. "I've heard of you, Mr. Bottoms." She pointed toward the shed like building. "You live over there?"

"Yes ma'am, I do. I hope you heard good things about me," he said with a sly grin. He waved his hand toward the tire. "Looks like you've had some bad luck."

"Nothing I couldn't take care of myself." She slammed the trunk lid together. "Were you inside the house in the last few minutes?"

"Goodness, no! I have no business in that old creepy house. It might fall on me."

"Have you seen anyone else around here in the last few minutes?"

He lifted his cap and scratched his head, as if he were trying to remember. "Nope. I ain't seen nobody all morning, except you and Hobe." His eyes narrowed. "You're lucky Hobe showed you around instead of old Zack."

"Are you talking about Mr. Zackery, Hobe's partner?"

"That's right. You know him?"

"No. I haven't met him yet. Is there something wrong with him?"

"You could say that." He cleared his throat, "He's mighty peculiar at times."

"Really." Tava, more concerned with the mystery person than with the peculiarities of someone she hadn't met, turned toward the old house, and told Rance about the intruder.

"You don't say!"

"It sounded like a man's footsteps," she added. "You didn't see him?"

"No. I called out. When he didn't answer, I hid."

"Where did you hide?"

Tava felt uncomfortable disclosing the hiding place to someone she'd just met. She shrugged. "There's plenty of places to hide in that old house."

"You're right." Rance cocked his head. "Are you sure it was a person?"

"Of course, I'm sure." Tava, irritated, felt as if he were stringing her along.

The lines around Rance's eyes wrinkled in amusement. "I wish I had a dollar for every time somebody told me they had heard something in that old house.

"No, no!" Tava shook her head. This wasn't supernatural. Somebody was walking inside the house."

His voice rose. "You said you didn't see anybody!"

"That's right."

"Well, then how do you know it was somebody?" He grinned out of the corner of his mouth.

"I would not be able to hear a ghost's footsteps, even if I believed in them." Tava noticed the expression on Rance's face and thought it was useless to try to convince him. No doubt he was a superstitious and ignorant man.

Rance pointed toward the house. "Where's the 'For Sale' sign?"

"I suppose Hobe took it back to his office." Tava explained the mix-up.

"I ain't never met your dad. Does he plan to buy this place?"

"He hasn't made up his mind yet."

"It's just as well." Rance stared down, digging the toe of his shoe into the damp ground. "There may be a lawsuit."

"A lawsuit!" Tava scrunched up her nose. "What for?"

"Over Cherohala, of course. Old Jess Henner has two grandsons, you know."

"No, I didn't know! I thought Uncle Jess's will was proper and legal."

"Maybe not." Rance shook his head. "Mrs. Trowbridge, Jess's housekeeper, told me the grandsons were not happy with the will. They think their grandpa was off his rocker, when he practically gave Cherohala to your dad."

"This is the first time I've heard that," Tava said, puzzling.

"There may be other things you ain't heard yet," he said.

Tava shrugged. Pepper lay on the ground nearby with his tongue lolled out. Rance bent over and stroked Pepper's back.

"I see Pepper has taken a fancy to you."

"Yes." Tava moved toward her car door. "Nice meeting you, Mr. Bottoms. I'm driving into town. Could I give you a lift someplace?"

"No, thank you anyway. If you need any help around here, just call on old Rance." He tipped his cap and ambled toward the shed-like house.

Tava watched him go, and decided he was hospitable, but strange.

Once again she ordered Pepper to go home. She slid into the car, her mind stuck on the mystery intruder. She swung the car onto the pitted blacktop road. It scooped through the greening countryside, around lonely pine studded hills, and rural homes. The road ended at an intersection in the quiet little town. She stopped at Jim's Garage, the first service station she saw, and dropped off the flat tire. The young bearded attendant assured her it would be ready to go back on the car in less than an hour.

Driving away she decided to look for the Realty Office to find out if someone else had a key to Cherohala. It was next door to Whitehead and Whitehead; the law firm that handled Jess's estate. Elisa Rhodes, the attorney, worked there.

When Tava thought of her, she thought of Shane's latest conquest, according to Hobe. She experienced a pang of jealousy and quickly reproached herself. Tava parked across the street from the Realty office and walked over. Her heart throbbed with the hope she'd run into Shane. Her resolve of no more romance was beginning to weaken as she entered the building.

A dignified older man with gray hair, wearing glasses and dressed in a blue striped suit, sat at his desk. She introduced herself.

He stood up. "I'm John Zackery. Call me Zack," he said with a broad grin, and held out his hand. After a firm handshake, he asked, "May I help you?"

Tava decided Rance's unflattering description of Mr. Zackery didn't seem to fit. "Is Hobe around?"

"He stepped out awhile ago. He should be back any minute now," Zack said, checking his watch. I suppose you've been busy looking around Cherohala?"

Tava nodded, intending to tell him about the intruder, but hesitated to repeat the incident to someone she's just met.

"There's still some fertile bottomland left out there," he said, "But the old house is in ruins. According to Hobe, it should be bulldozed, along with the rickety barn and Rance Bottoms' shack."

Tava drew back aghast. Destroy Cherohala! The very idea! She turned slightly; biting her lip to keep silent, and suspected why Rance and Zack weren't friends. Rance would be left without a home!

Hobe entered and called out, "Hi Tava. You missed a great lunch. Clam chowder was the specialty of the day."

Tava turned to Hobe. "One of my favorites."

"Are you all through examining the inside of the old house?"

"Not quite," she said, hesitating.

"I figured you'd be at the old house all afternoon. What can I do for you?"

She blurted out the frightening experience at the house. Zack gaped, and turned toward Hobe who was grinning in disbelief.

"Does anyone else have a key?" she asked.

Zack pointed to Hobe. "Ask him. He's in charge."

Hobe shrugged. "Not unless Shane has given it to somebody."

"Someone has a key!" Tava argued. "It had to be a man because of the heavy footfalls."

"But you didn't see him!" Hobe smiled and patted Tava's arm patronizingly. "You thought I was teasing about the Ghost of Cherohala, didn't you?"

"I still do," Tava quipped.

Hobe laughed, and then turned serious. "Did you see a car?"

"No. I did see Rance Bottoms. He denied he was in the house."

"So it wasn't Rance. Did you lock the door after you went inside?" Hobe asked.

"Yes. I heard Pepper scratching on the door, and unlocked it for him, but I relocked it. The person had to have a key. Both back and front doors were locked when I came downstairs."

"Hmm." Hobe frowned. "Sometimes one forgets if he locks or unlocks a door, but I'm not saying you did. Shane's been showing the place, but he didn't mention loaning a key to anyone."

He turned to Mr. Zackery, who was at his desk. "Zack, did we loan anyone a key to the old Cherohala house?"

Zack shrugged. "Not that I know about."

Hobe turned back to Tava. "He could have entered through a window."

"But I heard a door slam."

"It could have been an inside door."

Tava thought for a second. "You're right. It could have been."

"Was anything messed up or missing?"

Tava shrugged. "I was scared half to death, and I didn't stay around to check."

Hobe appeared surprised. "Of course, you were scared! It's strange someone would wander into an old house and not answer you."

"I feel he had a reason," Tava said.

"Whatever purpose," he said. "If I were you, I wouldn't go back inside that house alone."

"You're probably right," Tava said.

"I'll call Elisa Rhodes. She'll send someone to check on the house's windows," Hobe said.

"Thank you," Tava said and told him about the lawsuit rumor Rance had mentioned.

"I heard that, too. I talked with Elisa about it. It was news to her. But that doesn't mean it isn't true."

He glanced toward Mr. Zackery. "Have you heard about it?"

"No." Mr. Zackery stood up, and reached for a gray felt hat on a wall peg. He put it on, and said, "I wouldn't doubt it. The will did seem a bit unfair. Now it's my lunch time." He glanced back, clipped his sunshades onto his glasses, and ambled toward the door. He waved. "It's nice to have met you, Tava."

"You, too," she nodded and furtively glanced around the office once more in case Shane had returned through a back door. Not seeing him, she gave up, and said, "I must be going also."

"Don't forget to pass my message along to your dad," Hobe said.

"I won't," she promised, feeling it was a disagreeable task.

Outside, Mr. Zackery waved to Tava through the tinted windows of his old green Crown Victoria. Tava waved back, labeling Zack an ignoramus when it came to preserving old family mansions. She returned to her car, thinking she had accomplished one thing by stopping at the Realty Office. No one else should have a key to Cherohala. But someone did. She knew she didn't hear a ghost. She opened her car door, and glanced up the street. Her heart skipped a beat at the sight of Shane striding along.

He waved to her. Dressed in khaki trousers, a plaid shirt with a burgundy tie, he called out in a cheery voice, "Hi, Tava."

Her face flushed.

"Hello, Shane."

"I'm sorry I didn't get to show you Cherohala."

"I'm sorry, too."

"Have you had lunch yet?"

"No." She had completely forgotten about food after the excitement of the morning. She was ready to go with Shane, although she wasn't hungry.

"Great!" Shane said. "How about joining Elisa and me?"

Tava's body stiffened at mention of Elisa. "Uh...let me think about my plans," she stammered, not sure how to respond.

"Elisa is a friend of mine, and an attorney with Whitehead & Whitehead law firm." Shane pointed toward the Law Office.

"Yes, I know," Tava said. "I met her over the phone."

"I'll dash in and get her."

"Wait! I can't go." Tava raised her hand haltingly. She wanted no part of a threesome. "I've got an errand to do. Thanks anyway." She forced a smile.

There was a look of surprise on Shane's face. "I'm sorry. If you change your mind, we'll be across the street."

"Thank you for asking me." Tava said, getting into her car. She stared after Shane until he disappeared into the building, then slumped down into the seat with a feeling of despair. Why had he asked her to lunch when Elisa would be there? Was he being polite or charming? Angry tears welled up in her eyes. She wiped them away quickly with a tissue; furious at herself. It was her own silly imagination doing her in. She had totally misread Shane's intentions.

She drove back to Jim's Service Station, and picked up the spare tire. The attendant had replaced the spare on the wheel. He commented he'd been unable to find a leak, and asked if she knew a practical joker that may have let the air out.

"No." She shook her head in surprise, and thought of the absurdity. Who would do such a thing! She could count on one hand the people she knew here and no one seemed to be a practical joker. On her way back to Aunt Kate's, she mulled over the attendant's comment. Had someone really let the air out of the tire? Although she didn't believe in ghosts for a crazy moment she almost thought that the ill fates of Cherohala were conspiring against her.

"That's pure nonsense," she said aloud, her chin up. She would never swallow that silly superstition. She squared her shoulders. Tomorrow would be better, she promised herself in an upbeat manner.

CHAPTER SIX

Imps of doubt gnawed at Tava's stomach when she burst into Aunt Kate's kitchen, smelling of spice and lemon. Would Aunt Kate believe the story of the intruder? Or would she shake her head and mark it up to a normal happening at Cherohala? Tava stifled an urge to pour out the events of the morning at once and tried to act nonchalant.

Aunt Kate, clad in a blue chambray dress, sat at the kitchen table. She sipped herbal hot tea from a white teacup. She wiped her mouth with a paper napkin. A portion of a tuna fish sandwich lay uneaten on a napkin atop the bright yellow floral tablecloth. Aunt Kate glanced up at Tava with a concerned look on her face. "Are you all right, dear?"

"Oh, sure." Tava stood in the middle of the room, and tried to mask her emotions.

"Have you had lunch?" Aunt Kate asked. "I have more tuna fish."

"No." Tava shook her head. "I'm not hungry."

"How about a cup of herbal tea?"

Tava nodded. "That sounds great."

Aunt Kate pushed her chair back, and started to get up.

"Sit still, Aunt Kate. I'll get it. You point to the right cabinet and I'll do the rest."

Aunt Kate turned and waved toward a corner wall cabinet. Tava whirled around, and bumped into a ladder back chair at the table. She opened the cabinet door, and took out a white teacup. She plopped in an apple cinnamon herbal tea bag and reached for the teakettle. She poured hot water over the tea bag. Her mind still in a muddle, she wasn't aware the cup was overflowing.

"Whoops!" Aunt Kate yelled.

Tava stopped and looked down. "I'm sorry! " Her face burned in embarrassment. "I've messed up your pretty tablecloth."

"Don't worry about it. I need a fresh one anyway." Aunt Kate blotted the overflow with a blue floral paper towel. "You must be upset over something. Is it Cherohala?" She shook her head. "It was pretty bad the last time I was there and it's been awhile. Please tell me why you're upset, honey."

"Not the condition of the house." Tava yanked out a chair from the table, and sat down.

"It's something else then? You don't have to tell me, unless you want to get it off your chest. I'm a good listener."

Tava nodded.

"How did you and Shane get along?"

"He didn't show me the house. He was out with his girl friend, Elisa Rhodes. Hobe Yates showed me around."

"Well, Hobe's a nice man, I suppose. He's a friend of Dottie's."

"Yes, I know." Tava removed the tea bag from the cup. She was unable to bottle up the intruder episode and the flat tire any longer and blurted out both frightening experiences.

Aunt Kate stared aghast and clapped her hands. "I'm thankful you hid in the armoire. At least it was good for something. It might have saved your life, honey! You say you heard a man's heavy footsteps? No doubt he was coming for you! When he didn't find you, he let the air out of your car's tire!"

"Do you have any idea who it could have been?" Tava asked.

"Goodness no! But you never can guess who is traveling along Ball Play road."

Tava reached across the table and patted Aunt Kate's hand. "Thanks for believing me."

"Why shouldn't I believe you?"

"I'm sorry. I thought, because of all the tales about Cherohala, you might not."

"This is different." Aunt Kate pursed her lips. "It seems a person's not safe anywhere now. Hobe shouldn't have left you alone!"

Tava sipped her tea. "I insisted he go to lunch. I met Rance Bottoms afterward. He didn't believe my story."

"Don't let that upset you." She waved her hand. "Rance can be ornery at times."

"Do you think maybe a homeless man who wandered in?" Tava asked.

"Why would a homeless man wander in Cherohala that time of the morning? There's no food to be found there." Aunt Kate thought for a second. "It must have been someone who was familiar with the old house. Whoever he was, he was up to no good."

Tava related the rumored lawsuit.

"What!" Aunt Kate looked astonished. "I hadn't heard that. I believe Jess's mind was clear when he wrote the will. The lawyers must have thought so too."

"Would it be unfair to the grandsons if my dad bought the place?"

"They weren't grandsons to Jess." Aunt Ruth propped her elbows on the table. "Less than a year after Jess, Jr., died, his widow remarried and moved away. Her new husband adopted the boys. Jess tried to keep in touch. Wrote letters and sent money. Never even received a thank-you note. After a time, he stopped writing. I don't believe he ever heard from the grandsons again - unless it was a graduation announcement - then he sent a little money."

"How cruel!" Tava said. "But it wasn't the grandsons' fault."

"I know. I reckon that's why Jess left his meager savings to them. Except for a small sum he left Mrs. Trowbridge, his housekeeper."

"And, of course, the option to buy Cherohala to my dad."

"Yes. Jess probably figured the grandsons wouldn't be interested in the old house." Aunt Kate said.

"Do you think Jess hoped my dad would save Cherohala?"

Aunt Ruth tilted her head. "Perhaps. Why else would he have held onto the old relic, when he had many good offers for the land. He could have taken the money and gone into a lovely retirement home."

"I'm glad you told me about the grandsons. My dad had mentioned Uncle Jess grandsons. But he didn't know anything about them. Now I've got to convince my dad to buy Cherohala, despite its condition and the rumor of the lawsuit," she said.

"Why do you really want Cherohala?" Aunt Kate asked. "I fell in love with the old place. I suppose I want to renovate it and make it lovely again. Perhaps it's this underlying need to be creative."

"I never expected you to succumb to the spell of Cherohala. If it makes you happy, hold onto your dream." Aunt Kate stood up, pushed the chair back, and yawned. "It's about time for my afternoon nap. Why don't you go upstairs and rest awhile too."

"I'm too hyped up. I think a walk would be better."

Aunt Kate nodded. "Good idea."

"Maybe Pepper would like to come along," Tava said. "You couldn't keep him from going. He's outside right now. Usually he stays near my feet."

Tava decided the shoulder bag would impede her walking and left it in the upstairs' bedroom. Outside in the yard, Tava whistled for Pepper. He was snoozing under a lavender lilac bush in full bloom. He leaped up, raced over, tail wagging, and followed Tava. She remembered her cell phone was in her purse, but decided not to go back for it. Surely nothing would happen on a rural road. She chose to go west in the opposite direction of Cherohala.

She strolled aimlessly along the narrow Ball play Road under a canopy of puffy white clouds, the sun in her face. Pepper trotted at her feet at first, then sped ahead. He darted in and out of the matted fields where dandelions and buttercups intermingled with red clover. The road curved around an old hilltop graveyard on the right. Tava's curiosity overflowed. She left the road and clambered up the grassy knoll to the cemetery.

Clumps of weeds, vines and bushes clogged the wire enclosure of the burial ground.

Was it a family plot, she wondered? She entered through a rusty wire gate, hanging awry. To get a better look, she waded through the tangled growth. Right off she recognized it as the Henner family plot from the names on the tombstones. She assumed the other names were Henner relatives. Immediately she found the double tombstone of Big Erk and wife, Ada. Isaac and his wife, Elizabeth, were buried nearby. Where were David and Horace's tombs?

Tava poked among the weed-covered stones for their names and read the epitaphs: "Gone But Not Forgotten, A Loving Husband, Married For Fifty Years, and Together Forever." Some stones were so worn only traces of names and dates remained. She noticed the death dates...most were decades old. Even the dates on the latest looking stones were well over a generation past. Had the neglected burial grounds been closed? She wondered if anyone, except Aunt Kate, remembered the interred. Had she overlooked David and Horace's markers? Or had they been buried elsewhere? She shrugged and turned to leave. She walked toward the gate, and stumbled over a leaning stone, half hidden among morning glory vines. She stared down, and jerked the vines away.

"It's Horace's stone!" she said aloud, crouching down.

She traced the faint chiseled name and date on the marker with her finger. David's tomb was not there. Had hard feelings occurred in the family after David had slipped off and joined the Confederacy? The War Between the States could have left bitter feelings in the family. Surely even a rebel son would have been laid to rest in the family graveyard. Aunt Kate would likely know.

She straightened up, and gazed at the tombs of her ancestors. A sense of belonging stirred inside. She realized this must be the reason many people found the hobby of genealogy fascinating.

A soft rustling sound distracted her. The noise came from the thicket outside the fence. She glanced around. Was it an animal weaving in and out of the underbrush? It had to be Pepper; Tava chuckled, and whistled for him. He did not appear, but the stirring ceased. Was Pepper sniffing out the scent of some little animal? Without further thought, she headed back to the blacktopped road.

Tava crossed over to the left side of the road and again whistled for Pepper. He bounded out of the bushes. There was no way Pepper could have gotten from the Cemetery hill to the other side of the highway without her noticing. She had mistaken another animal for Pepper. She laughed softly to herself.

THE SPELL OF CHEROHALA

At the sound of a car motor, she moved to the edge of the road. An older model green Ford swerved around the curve at a dangerous speed. She leaped off the road into a drainage ditch and squinted open-mouthed at the speeding car. Its tinted windshield, and the sun in her eyes kept her from seeing the driver, who wore a hat and sunglasses. The car looked exactly like Mr. Zackery's. Why would he speed recklessly on a narrow country road? Pepper dashed off across the field again.

No sooner was the car out of sight, when it returned going in the opposite direction. Tava stood trembling in the weedy drainage ditch, and wondered what was going on. The car barreled off the roadway straight toward her in the ditch.

She screamed and leaped onto higher ground beside a barbed wire fence. Her heart thumped wildly. It seemed someone was out to get her she realized with horror and glanced back. The car swerved back onto the roadway and raced away. For a second Tava stood numb. Then she began to shook and heave. It was a good thing she hadn't eaten lunch. When her senses returned she clapped her hands to her face! She had failed to get the car's license number. Everything had happened too quickly. The question haunted her. Had the driver been Mr. Zackery? If so, why had he tried to run her down?

A pain shot through her right ankle, as she leaped back to the roadway. She bent over and rubbed the ankle. Was it sprained? With the roar of the car echoing in her ears, she knew there wasn't time to bother about it now. The car might return any moment. She took to her heels and fled. Pepper materialized from the bushy roadside, and raced along.

Tava didn't slow down or stop until she reached Aunt Kate's yard. She rushed into the house, slamming the door, eager to tell her about Mr. Zackery. She panted loudly, and paused in the foyer to catch her breath.

When she saw Aunt Kate's bedroom door closed, she hesitated, knowing she was still resting. Should she call someone? The Sheriff? What could she tell about the driver of the speeding car who tried to run her down? Not much - only the color of the car and not the license plate number. She suspected Mr. Zackery, but she couldn't be sure. In her uncertainty, it might be useless.

There was nothing left to do but go to her room. She'd tell Aunt Kate later. She hobbled up the stairs, still shaken up from the narrow escape. She paused on the landing, and thought back. Had Rance been trying to tell her something, when he described Mr. Zackery as peculiar?

She lay down on the bed, closed her eyes, and tried to relax. She could hear the squeal of the tires, and the roar of the motor. Why was some one after her? Was there something about Cherohala that she did not know!

CHAPTER SEVEN

A sharp rap on the bedroom door awakened Tava from a restless nap. "Yes," she called out.

"It's dinner time," Dottie called.

"I'll be down soon," Tava muttered. She rose, rubbed her eyes, and sat on the side of the bed. The harrowing experience came to mind. The specter of the speeding car still hung on. She shuddered and wondered who targeted her, and why? Had the culprit mixed her up with someone else? Had he been the intruder at the old house, and the one who had let the air out of her car tire? Was he out to get her? How could her presence threaten anyone?

She remembered the pain in her right ankle and stretched out her leg. She reached down and felt it. It didn't appear swollen, and the pain had subsided. Perhaps it was a superficial sprain. She arose from the bed, hurried across the hall to the bathroom, and freshened up. She stomped down the stairs to the dining room. Aunt Kate and Dottie sat in straight back dining chairs, waiting for her.

"Do you feel rested now, Tava?" Dottie asked. Tava, still in an apprehensive mode, and eager to tell about someone trying to run her down was taken aback at the question.

"Rested? That wasn't my problem."

"Oh." Dottie said. "Aunt Kate takes a nap every afternoon. But you can't do that, can you?"

"Not since I was in kindergarten." Tava shrugged.

"I skipped lunch today, but I still don't have an appetite."

"Tava, You're probably still upset over what happened at the old house today," Aunt Kate said, and turned to Dottie.

"She had an intruder. Then a flat tire."

"Uh..." Tava started to speak.

Dottie interrupted. "Hobe came into the bank today and told me about the intruder. That sounded scary and he didn't mention the flat tire."

"I forgot to tell him about it when I was in the Realty Office today,"

Tava eased down into a dining chair at the table. She needed to tell them what happened to her before the nap.

"Some one tried to run me down on my walk."

Aunt Kate and Dottie stared with open mouths at Tava.

"Who tried to run you down?" Dottie asked with a concerned look.

"I don't know for sure."

Aunt Kate put her fork down. "Where did you walk?"

"I walked on the Ball Play Road." Tava said.

Dottie sat up straight. "Where on the Ball Play Road?"

"Near the Henner Family Cemetery."

"Can you describe him and what kind of car he was driving?" Aunt Kate asked.

"He drove an old model green Crown Victoria and wore a gray hat and sun glasses."

"Did you get his license number?" Dottie asked.

"No. I was too upset and running. I didn't take my cell phone with me because I didn't think there'd be a need."

"It sounds like you're describing Zack." Dottie said.

"That's what I thought," Tava agreed.

"I cannot believe Zack would do such a thing!" Dottie said.

"Neither can I," Aunt Kate sounded adamant.

"I think you should call Sheriff Greene," Dottie urged.

Aunt Kate suggested, "Why don't you go ahead and eat before the food gets cold and then call."

Tava didn't feel hungry, but the aroma of the food overwhelmed her. She took a slice of roast beef, topped it with a bit of hot gravy. By the time she added new potatoes and green peas, she still hadn't worked up a desire to eat.

"Tava, I wish you could eat something. How about a buttered roll?" Aunt Kate passed them over.

Tava took one. "Thank you." She bit into it, and laid it on her plate.

"You said you walked to the family cemetery," Dottie said. "Did you go inside, and look around?"

"Yes, before I was almost run down."

"Oh," Dottie exclaimed, "I must go there one day. Aunt Kate, you're probably the only one who remembers anyone in that cemetery."

"Most likely," Aunt Kate said with a somber look. "I reckon I'm the oldest Henner left."

Tava pushed her plate back.

Dottie said, "I see why you have no appetite, Tava. The flat tire, an intruder in Cherohala, and being almost run down!"

Aunt Kate's face paled. "You poor dear! And to think I was resting in my room, when you returned and unable to comfort you."

"Something is going on around here, and you seem to be the target!" Dottie said.

"I think so, too," Tava said. "It's not a good feeling."

"Perhaps someone is trying to scare you away, but not kill you," Aunt Kate said.

"That's what it sounds like Tava, " Dottie agreed.

"But why?" Tava asked. "Could it be Cherohala?"

"Yes." Dottie stared at Tava.

"Hobe mentioned something like that when he suggested we have lunch." Tava said. "He said some relatives might resent me."

"That could be possible." Aunt Kate nodded.

"Everything points to Zack," Tava said. "When I met him earlier today he thought Cherohala should be torn down."

"It couldn't have been Zack!" Dottie adjusted her glasses. "He wouldn't do such a thing!"

"Dottie's right." Aunt Kate gestured with her hands. "Zack's not that sort of person. I've known him most of my life."

"I'm glad to hear that," Tava said. "I suspected him because of the car, his gray hat and sunglasses." Then she repeated the remark Rance Bottoms made about Zack.

Aunt Kate thought for a moment. "Rance doesn't like Zack, because he wouldn't sell him a piece of land on credit. Poor Rance has very few friends."

"That old model Ford car is common around here," Dottie said. "It wouldn't be unusual for someone to have a car similar to Zack's."

"Right," Aunt Kate agreed.

"The driver could have lost control if he were speeding," Dottie said.

"No." Tava raised her voice. "He came after me twice."

"Why don't I call Sheriff Greene for you, Tava? You're probably still upset." Dottie reached over and picked up her cell phone. After she ended the conversation, she turned to Tava. "The Sheriff will get in touch with Zack as soon as possible. That's all the Sheriff can do at the moment."

"Thank you for calling," Tava said, unable to shake her apprehension.

"If it had been a BMW, it would have been Hobe for sure." Dottie laughed. "He's the only one around here that has one. Hobe seems to be an asset to this area. He came here about two years ago and fit right in. He's a relative of Zack's or perhaps Hobe's late wife was. Zack took him in and soon after made him a partner in the real estate business. Hobe joined all the civic organizations and tries hard to be one of us."

"I don't think Hobe believed my story about the intruder," Tava said.

Dottie laughed. "He teased you, huh? That's his personality."

Tava sensed Dottie's defensive attitude toward Hobe. Dottie giggled. "I sound like a PR person when I described Hobe. I was only trying to clarify his reputation. He's thirty-five or so. Too mature for you, Tava."

"You're right." Tava grinned, and suspected Dottie was interested in him.

Dottie waved her hand toward Tava. "You probably feel like packing up and going home after a triple whammy on the same day!"

"Absolutely not!" Tava vowed. "The incidents may not have been connected. But I believe someone resents me and wishes I'd leave."

"You must be on guard from now on, and never go out alone." Aunt Kate said.

"For the life of me, I can't think who would resent you. Who around here would want Cherohala?"

"I've been curious to know where you hid in the old house when you heard the intruder," Dottie said.

Tava told her.

"Really!" Dottie's face brightened. "I must see that piece of furniture."

"That armoire has been around a long time," Aunt Kate said.

"I'd love to see all the furniture in Cherohala," Dottie said. "In fact, I've been thinking I'd get permission from Hobe to go inside the house."

"Hobe told me you were interested in Cherohala," Tava said, her feelings warming toward Dottie. "Do you like antiques?"

"Yes!"

"Then we're kindred spirits." Tava laughed.

"Indeed we are." Dottie pushed her plate back. "I'm a member of East Tennessee Historical Society and well aware of Cherohala's historical significance. The Society is interested in the old mansion, but there is little we can do now. Do you know Cherohala is listed in the United States Government's National Register of Historical Places?'

Tava caught her breath. "Really! That's another reason the old house is worth saving."

"You bet." Dottie nodded. "Cherohala was built solidly to last for generations. I believe it can be renovated. Don't let anyone tell you differently."

"Won't it take more money than it's worth to restore it?" Aunt Kate asked.

"Who can put a price on historical places!" Dottie said.

Aunt Kate shrugged. "I reckon I can see your point."

"Guess what!" Tava's eyes sparkled. "I have the keys to Cherohala. When would you like to take the tour, Dottie?"

"As soon as possible," Dottie said. "How about you, Aunt Kate?"

"I don't know." She appeared to be in a quandary. "What if that prowler returns?'

"I won't go back into the house alone," Tava said. "But I can't let that incident keep me from doing what I came to do. When we get inside, I'll lock the doors, and check all the downstairs windows. We'll have our cell phones."

"There'll be three of us, if you go, Aunt Kate," Dottie said. "There's safety in numbers."

"Well, I reckon I can go. Although the house holds such sad memories,"

Aunt Kate said thoughtfully. Then she brightened. "It's furnished in antiques, you know."

Tava scrunched her nose. "I saw very few pieces."

Aunt Kate frowned. "You mean they're not antiques!"

"No, I didn't mean that," Tava said. "Most of the furniture is gone. I saw a lowboy chest in the foyer the day I arrived. It's not there now."

"What!" Aunt Kate looked dumbfounded. "The house was full of furniture the last time I visited Jess!"

Tava spread out her hands. "Jess must have sold the furniture or given it away."

"Jess would have never sold the furniture!" Aunt Kate shook a finger. "Neither can I imagine him giving it away!"

"Just my luck to miss seeing the antiques." Dottie scowled.

"All is not lost, Dottie," Tava said. "The armoire is still there and a few other pieces. When can we go?"

"I'll take Thursday off from work. I have a day coming anyway," Dottie said.

"Good," Tava said. "Is Thursday all right for you, Aunt Kate?"

"Any time is all right." Aunt Kate arose from the table, still visibly upset, and mumbled something about the furniture to herself.

The phone rang. Aunt Kate hurried to answer it. She picked up the receiver and turned to Tava. "It's for you."

Tava, thinking it was her mom or dad calling, scrambled up from the chair. She couldn't wait to tell them that Cherohala was listed as a Historical Place. She picked up the phone. It was Shane.

"Shane!" Tava repeated enthusiastically; her hands trembled. "How're you?"

"Great! I heard you had a scare today at Cherohala."

"Right," Tava said with a nervous giggle.

"Are you feeling all right now?"

"Uh…I survived. Tava started to relate the speeding car episode, but decided against it. At that special moment with Shane on the phone its importance diminished. She tried to sound casual, and lied, "I'm okay now."

"Did you eat lunch today?" he asked.

"No."

"You made up for it tonight, huh?"

"I tried," she said.

"How about dinner with me tomorrow night? I know a super place to eat."

"I'd love to go," she gushed, putting aside the "no romance resolve," and any thought of Elisa. Her heart thumped wildly in anticipation.

CHAPTER EIGHT

Tava opened her eyes in the shifting rays of the morning sun. A vague feeling of uneasiness enveloped her. Where was she? Her sense of place returned. She was in Aunt Ruth's upstairs bedroom. She stretched and listened to the twittering of the birds outside the window.

When she noticed it was 8 A.M. by the clock on the bedside table, she popped up. She wasn't used to sleeping that late! What would Aunt Kate think of her? The edginess hung on as she slipped into her blue striped housecoat. Had she dreamed Shane had asked her out to a dinner date last evening? No, she hadn't dreamed it. She was certain it had happened. She smiled to herself, and distinctly remembered his voice on the phone. He had such a pleasant voice. Even now the memory of his voice sent delicious shivers throughout her body.

She became aware of what caused the apprehension while she showered. Her dad had not returned her phone call from last night. He had been out with a client, according to her mother. Had he gotten home too late to call? She must try again after breakfast. She must convince him how important it was to restore Cherohala. With only a week left on his option to buy the place, it was imperative he makeup his mind soon. In a positive way, she hoped. In all fairness she would tell him of Hobe's offer, and of course, mention his intention of destroying the ancestral home.

Tava slipped into blue jeans, a white sweatshirt, and bounded down the stairs. Aunt Kate, in a rose colored housecoat, sat at the table drinking coffee and reading the morning newspaper. An empty cereal bowl sat in front of her.

"Good morning, Aunt Kate," Tava called cheerily. "I'm sorry I missed having breakfast with you and Dottie. I don't know why I overslept."

"No reason for you to get up early." Aunt Kate put the paper aside. "Most likely you were stressed out from yesterday."

"I feel fine this morning." Tava waved her hands.

Aunt Kate peered over her glasses. "That's great. What would you like for breakfast? Dottie had waffles with strawberry jam."

"I'll help myself to cold cereal." She walked over to the counter top where different varieties of boxed cereal were stacked and chose the Oat Flakes. She emptied them into a bowl, added milk, and sat down across from Aunt Kate. Her thoughts still focused on Shane and their date that evening.

Tava finished the cereal, and put her dirty bowl into the dishwasher. She peered out the kitchen window at the profusion of spring flowers in the back yard.

"Aunt Kate, your daffodils, hyacinths, and tulips remind me of a giant Easter basket."

"Thank you, dear. I enjoy my spring flowers. I'm glad my hobby is working outside in them."

"This would be a good time for me to get out and do some sketching," Tava said.

"Sketch something for me," Aunt Kate said. "I need a bright picture for a spot in my dining room."

"Sure," Tava promised, and hurried upstairs to her room for the art materials. She came back carrying an overflowing tote bag and pointed. "I'll be out back."

Outside, Pepper followed Tava's footsteps across the lawn's dewy grass, glistening iridescently in the bright sun filled morning. Tava plunked the tote bag on the backyard redwood picnic table, and sat on the bench under a giant oak tree. She pulled out a pen, pad, and visually surveyed her domain. Pepper rested at her feet. Several gray squirrels scampered across the yard, and fed on the spill from the bird feeder nearby. They seemed oblivious to Pepper.

Tava gazed across the lawn to a hillock beyond and sketched a landscape scene. She added a splotch of golden daffodils. After a few moments, she paused, and stared critically at the picture. It wasn't up to par. Her strokes appeared too rigid. Was she still uptight from yesterday? Disgusted with her efforts, she snatched the drawing from the pad, wadded it into a ball, and flung it back into the tote bag. Leaning forward, she stretched her shoulders. The sunny morning had flown. In a few minutes she half-heartedly started another sketch. Around 11 o'clock Aunt Kate yelled from the back door.

"Tava, you have a phone call!"

"Coming," she answered, and glanced at her work. Despite the second attempt, the sketch wasn't her idea of a gift. She'd try again later. She dashed across the lawn and slapped her hand to her forehead. She had completely forgotten to phone her dad. Perhaps he was returning her call from last night. Or could it be Shane calling to tell her something had come up, and their date for the evening had to be cancelled? She grimaced at the depressing thought as she opened the back door.

Inside the kitchen Aunt Kate waved her hand. "You seem to be mighty popular around here."

"Who is it?" Tava asked.

Aunt Kate shrugged. "I don't have caller I.D."

Tava picked up the phone, hands shaking, and answered. When the caller identified himself as Hobe, she breathed easier.

After the usual pleasantries were over, Hobe asked, "How about that rain-check lunch date at the Lunch Box? Can you make it at noon today?"

Tava thought for a second. "Sure. Today would be perfect." She wasn't exactly enthused about a lunch date with Hobe, but her creative juices weren't flowing, and she needed something besides sketching to fill the day.

"I'll pick you up around noon," he said.

"No, no," she protested. "I'll meet you there at noon." It would be better if she were in control, she decided. Especially with someone she had just met. Driving her own car gave her that option. She repeated the gist of the phone call to Aunt Kate.

"That's a delightful place to eat. It's run by a group of ladies who have more time than money. Lunch is the only meal they serve." Aunt Kate grinned slyly. "It seems Dottie is wrong occasionally. Especially about Hobe being too mature for you!"

"Oh, no, Aunt Kate! This is not what you think." Tava shook her head. "It's only a business lunch, I believe."

"Uh, huh," Aunt Kate grunted, disbelief showing on her face.

"You've been here less than three days, and already you have dates with two of the town's most eligible bachelors and both on the same day! I'm not surprised. The Henners have always been go-getters. They usually wind up at the top of the heap or at least with the best mates."

Tava smiled, reveling in the fuss Aunt Kate was making. She had never had so much attention. She returned to the backyard, picked up the tote bag, and hurried upstairs to dress. She changed into a lavender blouse and a cotton madras skirt. Tying her hair back with a multi-colored ribbon, she slipped on a pair of espadrille shoes. By then it was time to go.

Tava found the restaurant easily, parked nearby, and entered. The dining area buzzed with noon customers. She glanced about for Hobe, but did not see him.

A middle-aged waitress with graying hair came up to her. "May I help you?"

"I'm waiting for someone," Tava said.

"Why don't you stand over there by the window?" The waitress pointed.

"Thank you," Tava said, and backed into a niche out of the line of traffic near the window. She stood staring out for a few seconds and felt conspicuous. She wished she had brought the sketchpad. She furtively eyed the noisy diners, who laughed and talked while eating. To pass the time until Hobe arrived, she noted the physical characteristics of a group of four young and attractively dressed ladies at the first table, socializing. She guessed they worked in business offices in the town. Fifteen minutes later Hobe slipped through the door. He was dressed fashionably in a lightweight gray suit, blue striped shirt, and a blue silk tie.

He spied Tava right off, waved, and walked over to her. "I'm sorry I'm late. I was with a client."

"I didn't mind the wait." Tava smiled.

Most of the diners appeared to know Hobe. They greeted him warmly, and several shook hands with his as he guided Tava to a reserved table by the window. He removed the sign and lay it flat on the table.

"They reserve this table for me every week day. I'm one of their best customers."

"Great." Tava said, and felt impressed.

A spray of jonquils in a cut glass vase adorned the table, covered with a red and white gingham cloth with matching napkins. The waitress, who had approached Tava earlier, reappeared with menus, and chatted briefly with Hobe. Tava ordered cream of broccoli soup, a garden salad, and iced tea. Hobe chose minestrone soup, a turkey sandwich, and coffee.

"I heard someone almost ran you down yesterday," Hobe said, over the din of voices, as they waited for their orders.

Tava stared at him with an open mouth. "Who told you?"

"I have eyes and ears everywhere."

He laughed. "Naw. I'm a kidder." He drummed his fingers on the tabletop. "You know how news spread in a small town."

"Yes, I know. Dottie tells you." They both laughed.

"Oh, no!" Tava clapped her hand to her mouth. "Dottie didn't tell you who I suspected it was, did she?"

Hobe broke into a grin. "She did."

He reached across the table and patted Tava's hand.

"Don't worry, Zack will never know."

Tava sighed with relief.

"Thank goodness. I'm sorry I accused him. But it looked like his car. Aunt Kate and Dottie set me straight. Do you know anyone else with a car like that?"

Hobe thought for a moment. "No. I can't think of anyone right now. Too bad you didn't get the license number."

Tava shifted her shoulders, and decided to hold back what she really felt; that someone was out to get her because she was a newcomer in town, or because she was interested in Cherohala.

Although it didn't make sense, it stuck in the back of her mind. Instead she said, "It was probably someone speeding, who had trouble making the curve."

"I suppose you're right." Hobe frowned. "But one can't be sure."

Tava sat up straight. "What do you mean? You think someone deliberately tried to run me down?"

"I don't know." He shook his head. "I was just thinking aloud."

"You've got me worried."

"Sorry about that. As a realtor I run into all kind of people. I've met a few who have strong feelings about property their families once owned."

"You mean some Henner relative, like the grandsons, might resent my being here, and looking over Cherohala. Or my dad's option to buy Cherohala?"

"Something like that."

"But I'm a Henner too."

"You're still an outsider. You've never lived here."

"I'm aware of that. Do you know a person who may feel like that?'

"I can't say that I do, right off." He shrugged. "I was speculating."

"If anything else happens to me while I'm here, I'm going to suspect a jealous relative," Tava said, losing her appetite.

"There you go." He guffawed. "What did your dad say about my offer?"

Tava frowned. She had forgotten to call her dad back before she came.

"Sorry, I wasn't able to get in touch with him. I'll try again after lunch."

"Don't go to any trouble on my account." Hobe held up his hand. "Why don't I call him?" He took out a pen and pad from his jacket's breast pocket. "Could I have his home and work numbers?"

"Sure." Blood drained from Tava's face as she rattled off the phone numbers. There was a possibility she could lose Cherohala if Hobe talked to her dad first. She became nauseous at the thought, and fidgeted. She glanced around the dining area for a private spot where she could call on her cell phone.

She didn't see a place, and decided to excuse herself and go to the rest room. At that moment the waitress brought their food attractively garnished with sprigs of parsley. Tava decided to wait until after lunch to make the call. She unconsciously wrinkled her nose, although the soup smelled delicious.

"What a face!" Hobe said. "Don't tell me you had another big breakfast."

"No." Her face reddened with embarrassment that her anxiety was showing so plainly.

"Is there something wrong with your soup?"

She swallowed a spoonful. "It's delicious."

Although her appetite was gone, she tried to act normal, and picked at the food. Hobe chatted about the restaurant's menus, and discreetly pointed out some of the town's leading citizens. Tava tried to appear interested in the conversation, but her thoughts were on losing Cherohala.

Near the end of the meal, Tava glanced up at a striking young woman, tall, willowy and brunette, who had entered the restaurant. She wore an elegant black tailored pantsuit, embellished at the neck by a red scarf. She turned in Tava's direction, showing poise and confidence in every gesture. When she saw Hobe, her eyes lighted up, and she hurried to their table.

Hobe scrambled to his feet, dropping his napkin, and greeted her. "Elisa!"

He held out both hands to her. "Join us for lunch."

He turned and introduced Tava.

"Hello, Elisa," Tava said and realized why Shane would be attracted to such a beautiful person.

"We've already met on the phone."

"So we have! Good to meet you in person." Elisa reached out for Tava's hand, grasping it firmly. "You'll be here a few days?"

"Yes." Tava nodded, trying to control her jealousy and reasoning Elisa and Shane weren't an item yet or Shane wouldn't have asked her to dinner.

Elisa motioned to Hobe. "Please sit down. I can't join you. I'm going to order a sandwich and eat it at my desk."

Hobe held out his hand in a solicitous gesture.

"No time to socialize?" Elisa ran her hand under her chin. "I'm up to here in paperwork. By the way, slave driver, where is Shane? I haven't seen him all morning,"

Tava stared at Elisa's smiling eyes. She liked her, despite feelings of rivalry.

"Come to think about it," Hobe said. "I haven't seen him either."

"Are you sure you didn't send him off to the boonies?" Elisa teased.

"No, but I would have if there had been land for sale."

"Excuse me, Elisa." Tava broke into their conversation, and repeated the rumored lawsuit over Cherohala.

"I've just heard about it too." Elisa nodded. "If it materializes, I'll be happy to work with you and your dad."

Hobe raised his hand. "If Tava's dad takes my advice, he won't need you, Elisa, except for legal transactions. I'll take Cherohala and its problems off his hands."

Tava's skin tingled at Hobe repeated offer.

"Hobe are you trying to ruin my law practice?" Elisa laughed softly, and with a wave of her hand, she turned to go. "See you later."

Hobe stared after her.

"She's charming, isn't she?" Tava said.

"She sure is," he said, glancing down, as if he had been caught with a wistful glint in his eyes.

"And Shane's girlfriend?" Tava asked casually.

Hobe looked up. "Who knows?"

Tava, surprised at his reaction, wondered if he were envious of Shane.

He reached across the table and encircled Tava's hand in his.

"I'm going to set you straight, my dear." He lowered his voice, and stared into her eyes. "Elisa is an attractive lady with a sweet personality, and an attorney. A good catch for some eligible bachelor. You're right up there with her...in fact, you're the beautiful one!"

Tava, taken aback, smiled, "Thank you."

She certainly basked in the compliment, even though it came from an a much older man in which she would ever have an interest. She casually withdrew her hand from his and arose from the table. "The meal was delicious, Hobe."

"Let's do it again soon," he said.

"Sure," Tava said, trying to appear gracious, but anxious to leave. "I've got to run."

"I hope to see you soon." He winked.

THE SPELL OF CHEROHALA

    Tava dashed out of the restaurant. Her heart clattered like a jackhammer. She raced to the car and yanked her phone from her shoulder bag. Cherohala was at risk.

CHAPTER NINE

Tava called her dad's work number. Luckily he was in and had not heard from anyone about Cherohala. He apologized for not returning her call, saying he had been Involved with a new client.

At once Tava recommended buying Cherohala, pouring out reasons, including its listing as a Historical Place. Her words tumbled one over the other. She reminded him of the option deadline, and reluctantly related Hobe's offer. Tava clung stubbornly to a ray of hope for Cherohala, and sighed with relief. She felt thankful she had gotten through first to her dad. She only hung up after her dad promised he'd decide in the next two days and assured her no decision would be made without discussing it further with her.

She returned to Aunt Kate's in the middle of the afternoon. Aware of her Aunts' naptime, she tiptoed through the house, and went directly to her room. Thoughts of the dinner date with Shane in a couple of hours sent a patchwork of frenzied emotions throughout her body. She hoped Shane was looking forward to the dinner date, also. Too tense to sketch, she settled for a long soak in the bathtub.

After the luxurious bath with a towel wrapped around her, she applied a smidgen of make-up. She dressed in a spring outfit; an ivory colored pleated skirt with a bracelet sleeved navy jacket, and beige heels. She shivered joyfully that she had the gumption to bring along a dressy outfit. She untied her hair, allowing it to hang freely about her shoulders.

At the sound of Aunt Kate and Dottie's voices, she clattered down the stairs, all fluttery, and joined them in the living room. Aunt Kate, sitting in an armchair, admired Tava's appearance warmly as she entered.

"Thank you," Tava said, all smiles, and eased down in the Queen Anne wing chair. Dottie, standing, wore a haggard after work demeanor. She tilted her head and waved her hand.

"Ah, Miss America! You look like you're chomping at the bits and raring to go?"

"You could say that," Tava grinned good-naturedly. She had gotten used to Dottie's cheeky remarks.

"Is the tour of the old house still on for tomorrow?"

"I certainly hope so!" Dottie said. "I took the whole day off."

She draped her pink cardigan sweater across a chair, and plopped down on the edge of the sofa.

"Was today as exciting as yesterday?"

"Nothing unusual, thank goodness," Tava replied.

"What!" Aunt Kate gasped. "Aren't you forgetting something, dear?"

Tava puzzled, and stared at Aunt Kate. "I don't think so."

"I'd have called it a fantastic day, if I'd had dates with two different handsome men!" Aunt Kate's eyes sparkled with mirth. "Only hours apart."

"Two different men!" Dottie gaped. "I know about the date with your cousin, Shane, but…"

"Distant cousin," Aunt Kate corrected.

"Whatever." Dottie waved her hand. "Who's the other one?" She glared at Aunt Kate, and then at Tava.

Tava hesitated, suspecting Dottie harbored unrequited emotions for Hobe. Her face burned, as if she were guilty of some misdeed, and stood in judgment before her grade school principal. She glanced toward Aunt Kate, whose face beamed. Was she going to answer for her?

"Oh. Did I speak out of turn?" Aunt Kate glanced up in a sneaky sort of way, and arose from her chair. "You tell her, Tava." She rushed from the room, muttering something about supper.

During the tense pause, Dottie stared at Tava. "Well, what's the big secret?"

"No secret." Tava shrugged. "Aunt Kate is making a fuss over the lunch date I had with Hobe. I'm sure he told you about it.'

"No!" Dottie scowled. "He came into the bank after lunch, but he didn't mention that he'd eaten with you."

"It was a business lunch. He wants to buy Cherohala from my dad,"

Tava said.

"All the more reason he should have mentioned it. He seemed to be in a hurry. Then there were several other people in there." Dottie arose from the sofa, picking up her sweater. "Don't worry about making me jealous. Hobe and I don't have that kind of relationship. We're good friends, and we share confidences. Or we did." She shrugged. "It teed me off when he forgot to tell me that Cherohala was on the market. Even though it was a mistake. Now he forgets to tell me he had lunch with my visiting cousin."

"He probably had something pressing on his mind," Tava said, thinking of the phone call he undoubtedly made to her dad.

"Whatever. My news source may dry up too." With a toss of her head, her shoulders slumped, Dottie walked toward her room.

Tava stared after her, feeling compassion. She hoped she hadn't jeopardized whatever relationship existed between Dottie and Hobe. She suspected Dottie made more of their friendship than he did.

At the sound of the doorbell, Tava leaped up, her heart hammering. It had to be Shane. She yanked the curtains aside, and peeked out the window. Shane stood on the porch. Ripples of joy spilled down her spine.

"I'll get the door," Aunt Kate called from the kitchen, and hurried down the hallway. She untied her apron strings on the way, almost colliding with Dottie, who had come out of her room.

Tava lagged behind, not wanting to appear too eager. Her heart beat pit-a-pat.

"Hello," Shane said to all of them. His face wreathed in smiles.

"Come in, Shane," Aunt Kate said, and motioned with her hand.

Shane, smelling of sandalwood aftershave lotion, appeared somewhat nervous as he stepped into the foyer. He wore a lightweight muted blue striped suit, a white shirt, and a blue patterned tie. He looked at Tava. "Ready?"

"Yes." She smiled and clutched her shoulder bag.

"You do have my door key, don't you, Tava?" Aunt Kate asked.

"I think so." Tava thrust her hand into the purse, and rummaged about, until she found it. She held it up.

"I'll wait up for you," Aunt Kate promised, and hovered solicitously over Tava.

"Hmm." Tava wrinkled her nose. "I don't know what time we'll be back."

She looked at Shane for an answer, since they hadn't discussed it.

He shrugged. "Whatever time you say, Tava."

"Aunt Kate!" Dottie boomed. "Aren't you forgetting something? They're adults."

Oh." Aunt Kate, seemingly disconcerted, covered her face with her hands. "Of course. I'm sorry, Tava. I don't know what came over me. I was treating you like a daughter."

"Like a teenager!" Dottie corrected.

"I'm not far past a teenager," Tava corrected.

Everyone laughed, breaking the tension.

"Go on, enjoy your dinner, and come back whenever you please – you are both adults!" Dottie said, and shooed them out the door.

Outside a gusty evening breeze ruffled strands of Tava's hair and blew it about her face. She smoothed her hair back, breathed deeply, and tried to still her thumping heart. Was this really happening, or was she imagining it all?

Tava settled down in the car, fastened her seat belt, and asked, "Where are we going?"

"The Hiwassee Club. I'm sorry I forgot to tell you," he said, and backed the car out of the drive onto the blacktopped road. "The restaurant is located on a lake, and the owners serve excellent food. Probably the best in the area." He rattled off several entrees. "Are you hungry?"

"Starved," she said, and remembered the lunch she had tried to eat. After a moment of awkward silence, she blurted out, "We're cousins, aren't we?"

He glanced at her with a surprised look and broke into a grin. "Of course. It almost skipped my mind. You see, I didn't grow up here. My parents moved back here when I was I high school. Somehow I never got around to meeting all the cousins. Sorry I didn't meet you sooner."

"I'm sorry too," Tava said. "I'm an only child. How about you?"

"Well…how shall I put it? I'm the only child of my parents. But, I have a brother and sister."

"You're fortunate to have siblings, but you'll have to explain that." She giggled.

"I'm adopted."

"Really! Then we aren't cousins after all." A warmth spread over her at the news.

"I'm glad, aren't you?" Shane flashed a smile.

"You bet! I wonder why Aunt Kate and Dottie didn't tell me?"

"They probably didn't know. My parents kept my adoption to themselves. They didn't tell me until I was eighteen. You know something. I wasn't entirely shocked when I learned. Things started to fall in place. I'd had recurring memories of another family, as long as I can remember, which I marked up to dreams."

"Really!"

"It's still hard for my parents to discuss the adoption. I don't know why. I could have never loved my biological parents more than my adoptive ones. Someday I hope to meet the ones who gave me life, if they're still living."

"Thank you for confiding in me," Tava said.

"When I tell you about my broken engagement, I won't have any secrets left." He laughed, and explained that he and his fiancée realized their mistake right off, and ended it, but remained friends.

Tava felt a quiet sense of relief he had opened up to her and realized he was a delight to be with. She couldn't remember when she'd been happier, or more excited, as they laughed and chatted together. Their likes and dislikes appeared similar also. Was this an unerring sign of love? Too soon the drive ended and their spirit of oneness was interrupted.

Shane reached out and grasped Tava's hand on the way into the restaurant. He squeezed her hand gently, caressing his fingers against hers. The unexpected contact sent shivers throughout Tava's body. She gazed up at Shane in open admiration. He beamed back. At that instant she knew their emotional chemistry was simpatico.

The Club's hostess met them at the entrance and led them into a pine paneled dining area. She seated them near a window overlooking a lake with placid waters.

Paintings of the area's natural resources - fishing, hunting, and boating decorated the walls. Flickering white candles, soft music, and the glow of a gas log in the fireplace heightened the cozy atmosphere. A young male waiter appeared with menus. He spoke to Shane in a familiar way implying he was a regular. Tava ordered grilled trout and Shane chose prime ribs.

While they waited for their food, Shane spoke eagerly of the area, filling Tava in on the dam, and the lakes with the many opportunities they provided.

Tava listened intently, charmed by his voice and gestures. She barely noticed when the waiter brought the delicately prepared food. During dessert, apple pie a la mode, Tava glanced at her watch.

She gulped in surprise and stared at the time. Where had the perfect evening gone? She looked about the room. They were all alone. She hadn't noticed the other diners leaving. In that magical moment she decided she must be in love.

"Shall we leave now, or let them kick us out," Shane said laughingly.

On the way to the car the thought of Elisa slipped into Tava's mind, marring their perfect occasion. She felt jealous and wondered how Elisa fit into Shane's life. She needed to know. Her feelings were at risk. On the drive back, she hesitated to ask, coward-like, afraid to hear or break the grandeur of the evening. She bit her lip, and promised herself she'd ask later.

"I'd like to show you the lake area,' Shane said, gesturing with his hands. "We have some great scenic spots, but I'm afraid you couldn't appreciate their beauty at night. Maybe we can drive out here during the day,"

"I'd like that." Tava's heart flip-flopped. Was he asking her out again? She waited expectantly for him to suggest a time, and was disappointed when he didn't.

"Hobe told me the terrific offer he made your dad for Cherohala," Shane said. "That is if he takes advantage of his option. Of course, you know about it."

A chill raced down the nape of Tava's neck and she wondered if her dad would succumb to some fabulous price.

"Yes, I knew Hobe was going to make an offer. I don't know the amount." She tried to choke off any emotion. "My dad would be foolish not to take advantage of his option. I suppose Hobe wants Cherohala for an investment."

"Probably." Shane said. "Will you be leaving soon, if your dad accepts Hobe's offer?"

"My original plan was to stay a week or ten days," she said. "But now who knows?"

"Your dad will be coming down soon then. He'll have to sign on the dotted line."

"Right," Tava mumbled, and lapsed into silence. Her stomach churned in a hollow feeling of apprehension.

After a few minutes Shane said, "You're so quiet all of a sudden. Are you all right?"

"I'm fine." She lied and tried to shake off the disturbing idea of losing Cherohala.

Shane reached over and tapped her on the shoulder. "Why not scoot over a bit closer to me."

"Sure." She quickly responded and cuddled her head against his shoulder in an unabashed affection. It was exactly what she needed to soothe her fears. His arm went around her, drawing her nearer. Their relationship was budding into a light romance. The closeness ended abruptly when Shane turned into Aunt Kate's drive.

On the way to the front door Shane tucked his arm around her waist. Tava responded by wrapping an arm about him. In the glow of the full moon and the cool night air, Tava became aware of Shane's vibrant body and felt comfortable.

Shane paused on the verandah and encircled Tava's waist with both arms. He pressed her gently to him and kissed her lips. Tava was filled with momentary dizziness, and her body tingled.

After the electrifying moment Shane pulled away. "Hey! It's been great."

"Right," Tava agreed and felt reluctant to let the evening go. Her heart raced like an engine.

"I hope to see you again soon," he said, and hurried to the car.

"You bet," She managed to answer, her eyes misted over with happiness. She unlocked the door and slipped inside. Not wanting to disturb Aunt Kate and Dottie, she carried her heels to avoid the clicking on the stairs, and padded up the stairway to her room.

Tava, awash in heart-throbbing emotions, doubted if she could sleep, as she changed into a pale blue nightgown. She sat on the edge of the bed and sighed. What a lovely evening. Suddenly it occurred to her. Why hadn't Shane asked her out again with a firm time and day? A dark thought clouded her thinking, and shattered the romantic mood. She sucked in her breath.

"Oh, no!"

Did Shane have an ulterior motive, the sale of Cherohala, for taking her out to dinner? He worked for Hobe. Had he been working for Hobe this evening? Numb, Tava lay down on the bed and closed her eyes in confusion. Was Shane being conniving? When she remembered his ready smile and the warmth of his arms, she couldn't quite believe it. It was hard to sort it all out in her mind.

She drifted into a restless sleep. A bizarre dream haunted her. In the dream Elisa and Shane held hands, sneering at her with haughty laughter. She reached out to them and they pushed her away with wild laughter and walked away arm-in-arm.

CHAPTER TEN

Thursday was a perfect day to explore the old mansion, Tava decided. The balmy morning air softened the greening spring. Despite a tugging uncertainty from last night's date with Shane, and apprehension from Hobe's pot-of-gold offer for Cherohala, Tava's spirits soared. Tava, dressed in mint green slacks and matching sweater, drove to Cherohala with Aunt Kate and Dottie. She parked in the driveway. As soon as she hopped out, Pepper came bounding toward her, his sides heaving.

"Come on, Pepper." Tava clapped her hands. Pepper rushed over, brushing against her legs, frisky like. She kneeled down and ran her fingers through his fur. "Glad you followed us, Pepper. It's no fun staying behind."

Straightening up, she trailed Aunt Kate and Dottie up the steps to the verandah. She paused at the front door, jiggled the house keys, and recalled the flat tire. Wheeling around she stared at her car. "I hope I don't get another flat."

"Are you sure the tire didn't lose air on its own?" Dottie asked. "I'm going by the mechanic's words," Tava said.

Aunt Kate shook her head. "I can't think of anyone who would do such a thing! Can you Dottie?"

"No," Dottie agreed. "I think the mechanic was wrong."

Tava shrugged and unlocked the door to Cherohala. Pepper crowded her ankles. "We might as well let him in too or he'll scratch at the door. I doubt if there's anything left he can damage."

"It's all right with me," Aunt Kate said, as Pepper dashed ahead into the old house. Tava relocked the door from the inside, and led them into the empty foyer. Aunt Kate gasped. "Where's the antique lowboy chest!"

"I saw it the first time I was here. The second time I came I didn't see it, and assumed I'd mixed it up with another place," Tava said.

"Someone has taken it?" Aunt Kate said, looking disgusted.

"Was it an antique?" Dottie asked.

"I'm sure it was," Tava said.

"Of course it was," Aunt Kate affirmed.

They followed Tava into the left parlor.

"Good heavens!" Aunt Kate exclaimed, and stopped in the middle of the floor, her hands on her hips.

"This room is almost bare! I know you told me the furniture was gone, but it's hard to believe."

She pointed to an empty space, and described a cabriole legged cocktail table that belonged there. "I wish I knew what happened to it!"

"We'll probably find out eventually," Dottie said, and wandered toward the dining room ahead of Tava.

Aunt Kate trailed. She threw up her hands in disgust over the missing china cabinet and dining table. "It's so unlike Jess to have given away his antiques."

"Could the grandsons have been right about Jess's senility?" Dottie asked.

Aunt Kate's eyes flashed angrily. "Absolutely not! Even if Jess had been senile, which he wasn't, the grandsons wouldn't have known. They never set foot in his house after they moved away."

In the kitchen Tava noticed a door she had overlooked on the first visit. She opened it and entered a small room. "This must be the pantry."

"The butler's pantry or work room," Aunt Kate corrected, following along.

"Jess stored a Singer pedal sewing machine and an antique Victor Victrola phonograph player in here." She gazed around the empty room.

"They're gone too," Dottie said.

"The last time I visited Jess before he died, I urged him to sell the house and everything in it. He didn't want to hear about it." Aunt Kate shook her head. "Stubborn man. I reckon he thought he'd live forever."

"Who would know what happened to the furniture?" Tava asked.

"Mrs. Trowbridge, his housekeeper, might know," Aunt Kate said. "Jess really depended on her that last year."

"Depended on her! Ha!" Dottie snorted. "I heard she hovered over him like a mother hen."

"That's true, but in a kind sort of way. I don't believe she'd have taken his furniture, because Jess paid her well," Aunt Kate said.

"Maybe Jess gave the furniture to her," Dottie said. "Sick or lonely elderly people often give their valuables to someone who cares for them."

"That's possible," Aunt Kate agreed. "Before we ask her, let's speak to Rance about the furniture."

"We can stop by and see him, when we finish here,' Tava said, and headed back into the kitchen. "If he doesn't know, could we visit Mrs. Trowbridge?"

"Sure," Aunt Kate said. "She lives about thirty minutes away. She'd be delighted to see us."

"I'm curious to know what happened to the antiques too, but I don't want to make a big fuss about it," Tava said, and headed toward the stairway. "I suppose Jess did what he thought was best."

Aunt Kate pursed her lips. "Jess was my brother, and I've lived near him all this time, so I knew his ways well. I have my doubts that he gave away the furniture."

On the second floor bedroom Dottie gaped at the bed with the tall headboard.

In the next bedroom Aunt Kate grumbled over the missing cannon ball poster twin beds.

Tava's favorite bedroom was the one with the armoire. She pointed out the piece of furniture to Dottie. "That's where I hid."

Dottie walked over, examined it, and opened its doors.

"Hmm," Aunt Kate grunted. "The armoire is out of place. Tava, push it away from the wall."

"Why?" Tava stared.

Aunt Kate waved her hand. "Go ahead. You'll see. It rolls on casters."

Tava leaned her shoulder against it.

"Wait," Dottie said. "I'll help you."

Together they rolled the armoire a short distance, and uncovered a door.

"Ah! A secret room." Tava giggled.

"No. A door to the attic," Aunt Kate said.

Tava opened it and peered into a narrow musty stairway.

"What's up there, Aunt Kate?"

"Most likely a lot of junk. I haven't been up there in years."

"I'll take a look." Tava clipped up the stairs with Pepper behind her. She paused at the top of the landing, and gazed around at the clutter.

"Come on up," she yelled. "It looks interesting."

The attic reeked of old, musty things. It overflowed with broken down chairs, loosely rolled woolen carpets, stern-faced portraits, barrels of yellowed clothing, heaps of old mildewed books, stacks of cardboard boxes, crates, and unrecognizable junk. Light splattered through a tiny dingy window curtained in spidery cobwebs in the rafters.

Aunt Kate climbed the stairs ahead of a puffing Dottie. "There's no telling what's stored up here. The house has always been in the Henner family. Some of this stuff may have belonged to Big Erk and Ada."

Pepper nosed about and scratched at a rolled up carpet.

"Stop it, Pepper," Dottie scolded. "You might destroy something valuable."

Pepper moved near Aunt Kate's feet, lay down, and nestled his head on his paws.

Tava heard a car motor that sounded nearby. Wary from the previous visit, she glanced toward the window.

"What does this window overlook, Aunt Kate?"

Aunt Kate shrugged. "It used to overlook the river."

"I doubt if you could see anything," Dottie said. "It looks like it hasn't been washed in a century. Besides you'd need a stepladder."

"I'll improvise," Tava said. Curiosity replaced her concern over the car motor. She noticed the crates, and slid one across the floor under the window. She stacked another one on top of it.

"Voila!" She waved her hand. "A stepladder."

"Careful now," Aunt Kate cautioned. "We don't want any accidents."

Tava yanked a fistful of blue tissues from her shoulder bag and nimbly clambered atop the crates. She held onto a rafter with one hand, and with the other, she swiped the tissues across the grimy windowpane. She peered through a cleared spot. "I can see the lake!"

Aunt Kate looked up. "I wish we could still see the river."

Dottie glanced up quickly, and continued rifling through the jumble.

Tava let go of her handhold and lost her balance. Teetering, she grabbed onto another rafter. Her fingers brushed against a metal-like object. She drew in her breath, steadied herself, and squinted up, wondering what she had felt. A rusty tin box, the size of a large business envelope, was lodged on a crossbeam. She snatched it, and climbed down.

"Look what I found!" She held it up.

Aunt Kate and Dottie stared.

"What is it?" Dottie asked.

"A rusty tin box." Tava tried to open it, but the lid was firmly stuck.

Dottie took the box and shook it. "There's something inside. I can hear a faint rustle."

Tava reached for it, and shook it again. Her imagination ran wild.

"Do you think it might be a map to the lost heirlooms?"

"I doubt it." Aunt Kate shook her head. "Most likely some kid hid it up there."

"There's only one way to be sure," Tava said, "I'll pry it open."

"Wait a minute!" Dottie warned. "Don't do anything illegal. The house doesn't belong to your dad yet."

"According to what Shane said last night, it may soon belong to Hobe," Tava said, feeling panicky at the thought.

"I don't see any harm in opening an old tin box," Aunt Kate said.

"Neither do I," Tava agreed. "I'll need a tool to pry it open. There's a tool kit in my car trunk." She dashed toward the stairs with the box.

"Stop, Tava!" Dottie shouted. "Wait until we finish here. Then you won't have to run up and down two flights of stairs."

Tava paused halfway down the stairs and conceded Dottie was right. "A good idea. I might as well leave it downstairs."

She carried it to the bottom of the first floor stairs and set it down, and then returned to the attic where Aunt Kate dusted portraits and rattled off family names.

Dottie poking through a barrel of clothing, yanked out a faded blue gingham bonnet, and tried it on. She cocked her head, and giggled. "How do I look?"

Tava grinned. "Not like a banker."

"If Hobe buys Cherohala, I hope he'll sell me the contents of this attic," Dottie said, dropping the bonnet back into the barrel.

"What would you do with this stuff?" Aunt Kate asked.

Dottie waved her hand. "I assume there's a lot of family history that should be donated to a museum."

"A good idea," Aunt Kate agreed. "There's no need for all this to be destroyed with the house."

Tava trembled inside at the mention of destroying Cherohala and her voice bristled with anger. "Hobe hasn't bought this place yet! If I have my way, he never will!"

Aunt Kate and Dottie stared at Tava.

"My! You sound determined," Dottie said.

Tava clenched a fist. "I am. Dad doesn't really want this place. If I can buy it from him, I'll turn it into a museum."

"A museum!" Dottie clapped her hands vigorously. "That's the best idea I've heard in a long time – it's just what we need. What do you think, Aunt Kate?"

"A museum?" Aunt Kate shook her head. "I'll have to get used to the idea."

"Buying Cherohala is probably a pipe dream," Tava admitted, but felt better for venting her anger.

"Forget the pipe dream part," Dottie said. "I liked you better when you were angry."

"Thank you," Tava grinned, and knelt down among the jumble. "Now I'm going to rummage about, and see what I can find." She opened a cardboard box, which overflowed with ledger books, cancelled checks, and legal looking documents. She flipped through some of them, musing over the life spans they represented. Aunt Kate and Dottie browsed the piles of junk.

Tava opened a humpback trunk, stuffed with bric-a-brac, and a packet of letters. She searched through the trunk, and found a piece of jewelry; a tarnished brooch with a turquoise colored stone. She held it up against her sweater.

"Isn't this pretty!"

Aunt Kate wrinkled her brow. "I recall someone wearing that pin."

"It might be valuable," Dottie said.

Tava dropped the pin back into the trunk.

Pepper, who was lying nearby, leaped up growling. His ears jerked up as if he were on guard duty. He gave a series of sharp barks. Then just as quickly, he settled back down.

"What's wrong with Pepper?" Tava asked.

Aunt Kate shrugged. Tava cocked her head and listened for a sound. When she heard nothing, she reached over and stroked him.

"Maybe he smelled a mouse or some other little critter up here," Aunt Kate said.

Dottie drew herself up. "If there's any mice up here, I'm leaving!"

"Don't worry, Dottie. Pepper was probably dreaming," Aunt Kate said.

Tava snatched up the packet of letters. One spilled out. She picked it up and read the name on the envelope.

"Aunt Kate, did you ever hear of Lavonia Henner?"

"Oh, yes. She was one of Erk Henner's daughters and lived in this house. Who's the letter from?"

"From Rance somebody. The last name is faded and it's hard to make out."

"Oh. Rance Goforth, of course. That was before my time. I've heard the sad story about them," Aunt Kate said.

"Another Rance. Is that a common name around her," Tava asked.

"No. Rance Bottoms is the only other one I know," Aunt Ruth said.

"Lavonia married Rance Goforth over the objections of her parents."

"What were their objections?" Dottie asked.

"He was from a Melungeon family."

"What are Melungeons?" Tava asked.

"A mixture of three races," Aunt Kate answered. "Native Americans, White, and African Americans. Lavonia was disinherited and then she and Rance moved away. Over the years the family lost touch."

"I never heard that," Dottie said.

Aunt Kate shrugged. "I reckon there are a lot of things you haven't heard. This mixing happened in this area of East Tennessee. Many people in that day were narrow minded and some still are."

"You must know all kinds of interesting stories about the Henner family," Tava said.

"I'll help you with the family tree anytime, the tales thrown in." Aunt Kate chuckled.

"You slipped up on one family story," Tava said, dusting off her hands and filled them in on Shane's adoption.

"No!" Aunt Kate gaped.

"I hadn't heard about it, either," Dottie said.

Tava remembered a question she had wanted to ask and nodded to Aunt Kate. "There's something I'm curious about. When I was at the cemetery I couldn't find David, the rebel son's tombstone? Did I overlook it or was he buried someplace else?"

Aunt Kate shook her head.   "No, he's not buried in the family cemetery."

"Where's that?" Tava asked.

"In the Little Tellico Church cemetery." Aunt Kate waved. "Not too far away."

"Did they bury him there because he fought for the Confederacy?" Tava asked.

"That's what it boiled down to, I believe," Aunt Kate said. "Bitterness over the war. It was difficult for most people to forgive at first. Big Erk and Ada's oldest son, Isaac, returned home from the war. The other two sons had been killed. The Henners were still in mourning and mixed up about their loyalties. Big Erk, although he loved David, reasoned since he had slipped away and joined the Confederates, it didn't seem fitting to bury him in the same cemetery as Horace. Of course, no one knew for sure which side Horace's killer was on. It was believed he was a deserter from one of the armies or he could have been a bushwhacker."

"I think I understand Big Erk's reasoning," Tava said. "But, I think it was sad."

"Yes, I agree," Aunt Kate allowed. "Later Big Erk changed his mind and decided to move David's remains from the Church graveyard to the Henner Family Cemetery. But he died before he got around to it." Tava shook her head. "I wonder why Ada didn't do it?"

"She had been against burying David in the church cemetery in the first place and vowed she'd have his remains moved to the family cemetery. For some reason she never got around to it either," Aunt Kate said.

Tears ran down Tava's cheeks after the story. Dottie seemed affected also and sniffed into a tissue. Aunt Kate shook her head and looked down.

"If I buy this house," Tava shook a finger. "I promise to have David's remains moved to the Henner family Cemetery."

Both Aunt Kate and Dottie stared at Tava, nodding in agreement.

"Another thing I plan to do when I buy this house is to have an attic party," Tava said. "We'll go through everything,"

"Hooray!" Dottie clapped her hands. "You'll put these records and mementos on display in the museum, I hope."

"It'll take people like both of you to turn Cherohala into a proper museum," Tava added.

Aunt Kate held up her hand. "I'm too old to get involved in something like that."

"No, you're not, Aunt Kate," Dottie said, and then turned serious.

"As much as I admire Hobe, I hope your dad doesn't sell him Cherohala. He'd have the house razed."

"That's why I want to buy it." Tava nodded.

"You're serious then," Dottie said.

"I've never been more serious," Tava said. "But, I can't compete with Hobe without money."

"Don't try to compete with him," Dottie said. "Appeal to your dad's family pride. You're his daughter for goodness sake! Surely you can think of something."

"Offer your dad a fair price," Aunt Kate suggested.

Tava held out her hands. "I wish I had the money."

"I'll help you get a loan at our bank," Dottie said.

"You will!" Tava sucked in her breath. "What can I use for collateral?"

"Cherohala, of course!" Dottie said. "Your next problem will be the funds for renovation. There may be a grant available. I'll look into it. If not, I'm sure I can talk some of our solid citizens into pledging their support. Perhaps they could become directors or connected somehow to the museum."

Tava blinked away happy tears and hugged Dottie. "How can I ever thank you!"

Dottie squirmed out of Tava's embrace.

"I'll be getting something too, you know. Perhaps I could become a partner?"

"Of course," Tava said.

"I must confess I had hopes someone would tear this old house down." Aunt Kate lowered her head. "And build a new one, so I'd have neighbors."

She glanced at Tava. "But, I'm coming around to your way of thinking. A museum might be a good idea."

"Thank you, Aunt Kate. You'd make a natural guide. You're chock-full of Henner history." Tava threw her arms around her.

"It would be something I could do." Aunt Kate grinned.

"We'd better finish up here before we get hugged to death," Dottie teased.

"We haven't seen the other rooms yet."

They closed the boxes and straightened up a bit. They returned to the second floor, and checked on the remaining rooms, which were almost bare.

Tava clattered down the stairs to the first floor with Pepper. Her emotions were on a high at the idea of buying Cherohala. She would call her dad at once and took out her phone. Dottie came down behind her.

Aunt Kate followed. "Where's the tin box, Tava?"

"Oh," Tava gave a start and twisted around.

"I left it at the bottom of the stairs." She backtracked, thinking she should have tripped over it, and stared at the spot where she had left it. It wasn't there. Frantically, she scanned the floor nearby. She became confused when she didn't see the box anywhere.

"Did you pick it up, Dottie?"

"Of course not." Dottie glanced around. "Are you sure you put it at the bottom of the stairs?"

"I'm positive."

Aunt Kate stared wide-eyed. "You don't reckon? Well, this old house does have a reputation!"

"Aunt Kate, you don't believe a ghost would steal a box that it could have gotten any time, do you?" Dottie giggled.

"You think I'm a stupid old woman, don't you?"

"I know you're not, Aunt Kate. I was kidding," Dottie said. "There has to be a reasonable explanation."

"I know," Tava said. "Someone came and took it. Like they took the furniture. That's why Pepper barked." Aunt Kate shuddered. "Maybe strange things do happen here."

Tava nodded, and unlocked the front door, "By human hands with a key."

CHAPTER ELEVEN

Tava, upset over the box's disappearance, walked silently out of the old house onto the verandah with Aunt Kate and Dottie. She paused at the bottom of the steps, and said, "Something's going on that I don't understand."

"I don't either." Aunt Kate shook her head.

Dottie seemed at loss for words.

"There could be a practical joker with a warped sense of humor or someone doing these things for another reason," Tava said. "What do you think?"

Aunt Kate shrugged.

Dottie wagged her finger. "Don't be too hasty in jumping to conclusions. Let's look at it rationally. Do you think Pepper could have carried the box off?"

"No." Tava shook her head. "He was with us the entire time and came down the stairs behind me. I would have noticed him." She glanced toward Pepper, who was sniffing in the grass.

"You're right," Aunt Kate said. "But I'm surprised Pepper didn't tear down the stairs after whoever it was."

"He did bark," Tava said.

"Pepper's getting lazy, spring fever, no doubt," Dottie added. "I have another theory about the missing box. Suppose Shane drove by, recognized Tava's car, and stopped. He assumed she was inside and entered. I suppose he still has a key. He may have called out. We couldn't hear him from the attic. Maybe he figured Tava was elsewhere on the property. He noticed the box, picked it up, and left."

"Yeah. That makes sense," Tava said. "I heard a car when we were in the attic." The idea that Shane cared enough to seek her out took some of the tenseness out of the situation.

"I'll give him a call later."

"With a little imagination, you can figure out most things," Dottie said, with a confident grin. "Hey! Let's don't stand here. Let's go see Rance, and ask him about the missing furniture. He'll know if Shane was here."

Aunt Kate nodded. "Let's walk over there, Tava. It's such a nice day. Rance lives only a hop and jump away."

"Sure." Tava fell in step with them on the pathway. The loss of the box had sidetracked her interest in the furniture.

"I was getting used to the idea of Cherohala as a museum, until the box mysteriously disappeared," Aunt Kate said.

"Perhaps there was nothing mysterious about it," Dottie said. "Rance may clear it up for us or the answer may only be a phone call away. Tava, I hope this doesn't affect your decision to buy the place."

"Definitely not. It would take more than a missing box to change my mind."

"I like your spirit!" Dottie said.

The door to Rance's shed-like residence was closed and all was quiet.

Tava hesitated. "Do you think he's home?"

"Knock anyway," Dottie urged.

Tava stepped onto the stoop and rapped on the door. There was only silence. She banged again much louder. In a few seconds she heard soft footsteps inside.

The door creaked open a crack. Rance peeked out. "Yeah!" he answered in a gruff voice. Wisps of uncombed graying hair tumbled over his forehead. His unshaven face puckered into a grimace as he squinted into the bright sunshine. A look of recognition crossed his face and he broke into an apologetic grin. "Morning. Didn't recognize you right off." He opened the door a bit wider, giving Tara a swift glance at his cluttered quarters.

"Good morning." Tava smiled.

Aunt Kate and Dottie chimed in with the greeting.

"Sorry to disturb you," Tava apologized, feeling uncomfortable over the intrusion. "We thought you'd be up."

"I'm up." Rance waved his hand. "Howdy Kate and Dottie. How've you been?" He pulled the door closed quickly and stepped onto the stoop with his red plaid shirttail hanging out.

Pepper raced up and licked Rance's hand. Without a word, Rance bent down and stroked Pepper's head.

"I don't know when I've seen you last, Kate!"

"It's been awhile." She nodded. "Drop in and have a cup of coffee with me sometimes. I'm usually home."

"I'll do that. I'd ask you ladies in but I'm an old bachelor and everything is in a mess." He guffawed and tucked his shirttail inside his trousers. "What can I do for you?"

"We've been looking through the old house." Aunt Kate turned and waved in Cherohala's direction. "Have you seen anyone over there this morning?"

"Shane, perhaps?" Dottie asked.

"No." He rubbed his eyes. "I didn't see you ladies either. I just got up."

He scratched his head in thought.

"Wait a minute. I may have got up earlier. Come to think about it, I did see a young fellow over there. No. I believe I saw him yesterday. I didn't sleep much last night. I'm still a bit confused."

"Who was the young man you saw?" Dottie asked.

"I didn't recognize him from here." He waved his hand. "Folks going to the lake take a short cut by the old house all the time. I never pay much attention to them."

Dottie turned to Tava. "If you buy Cherohala, you may have to put up a "No Trespassing " sign on the property."

Rance stared at Tava. "You're buying Cherohala!"

"I hope so."

"A sign would stir up trouble for you. Folks around here have been using that trail to get to the river for years," he said.

"I'd be sorry to make such an abrupt change," Tava said. "But the way things are going, it may be necessary."

"What do you mean when you say the way things are going?" he asked.

Tava told him about the missing box.

Rance shrugged, "There's plenty of cracks and crevices in that old house where a box could fall."

"It didn't fall," Tava retorted.

"Well a "Posted Sign" might be all right." Rance crossed his arms. "I need to sell my old rowboat anyway."

"Oh, don't do that. You'll be welcome to use the path," Tava said.

"Do you know anything about Jess's missing furniture?" Aunt Kate asked.

"His furniture is missing?" Rance appeared taken aback.

"Most of the good pieces," Aunt Kate said.

"Hmm." Rance fingered his jowl. "Let's see. Mrs. Trowbridge sent a man with a truck to pick up some of it."

Dottie nodded knowingly. "What did I tell you, Aunt Kate? I figured she got it."

"I wonder what happened to the other pieces?" Aunt Kate said.

Rance spat on the ground. "I have no need for furniture. I'm living here on borrowed time, you know." He glanced at Tava. "Why are you interested in old furniture?"

"I'm interested in antiques," she said. "I'm curious to see the furniture that was in Cherohala. Perhaps I can find similar pieces to refurnish the old house."

"Let's hope Mrs. Trowbridge can help us," Aunt Kate said.

"Thank you, Mr. Bottoms," Tava said, and turned to go.

"Just call me Rance. Everybody does."

Tava smiled. "Okay."

"I'm afraid I wasn't much help," Rance said. "You've got my curiosity aroused over that box. Let me know what you find out."

"Sure," Tava promised, her feelings softening toward him. Despite his ways, his impending homelessness touched her. Perhaps, if her dream of buying Cherohala came true, she'd consider his plight.

On the way to the car Aunt Kate suggested they visit Mrs. Trowbridge after lunch.

"A good idea," Tava called the Realtor's office on her cell phone, and asked to speak to Shane. He wasn't in.

"Did either of you get a glimpse inside of Rance's shed?" Dottie asked.

"I didn't notice," Tava said and opened the car door.

Dottie shuddered. "It looked like a pigsty! Everything piled together and covered up with sheets in that one big room."

"Don't be too hard on Rance," Aunt Kate chided. "He's probably doing the best he can."

When they were all seated, and belted up in the car, Tava noticed Pepper standing by eyeing them dolefully.

"Let's give Pepper a lift," Tava said. "Dottie, do you mind if he rides in the back seat with you?"

"If you don't mind the dog hairs, it's all right with me." Dottie said, and opened the car door for Pepper to enter.

Tava turned on the car ignition, but the motor didn't start. Puzzled, she tried again. After several attempts, she knew there was a problem.

"Do you think your battery is dead?" Dottie asked.

"It shouldn't be. I had the car serviced before the trip. Oops!" Tava slapped a hand to her forehead. Fear spread over her.

"I left the car unlocked while we were in the old house!" Aunt Kate gaped. "You think someone tampered with it?"

Tava gripped the steering wheel. "It looks that way."

Aunt Kate's face turned ashen. "Who could be doing this?"

"I wish I knew!" Tava stewed with anger.

"I can't believe anyone around here would do such a thing in this isolated place," Dottie said. "Unless it was that young man Rance saw over here. Then again, it may be simple mechanical failure."

"I hope you're right, Dottie." Tava choked to keep her voice steady. But there have been too many coincidences."

"There's more fishermen than you think who use this shortcut to get to the lake," Aunt Ruth added.

CHAPTER TWELVE

A faint breeze blew across Tava's troubled brow as she peered under the car hood. The array of engine parts appeared in order to her non-mechanical eye. She gave up quickly, not knowing what she was looking for. She turned to Dottie, who stood nearby with Aunt Kate. "Do you know anything about a car motor?"

"Good heavens, no."

"I'll have to call a service station for a tow truck," Tava said, with an air of resignation.

Dottie held up her hand. "Don't give up yet. Let's ask Rance to take a look."

"All right." Tava glanced wearily toward Rance's place. She flinched at the idea of returning there, and asking for help.

"I'll walk over and get him," Dottie volunteered, as if she sensed Tava's reluctance. "It won't hurt to ask. He might find the problem right off."

Tava nodded, and paced in front of the car, hoping the trouble was minor.

Aunt Kate poked about in the weedy grass, searching for lavender violets.

Shortly Dottie returned with a scowling Rance.

"I told Dottie I'm not a mechanic," he said, his voice edged in irritation. "I don't even own a car."

"Could you take a look under the hood anyway," Dottie urged. "You might notice something out of place."

"Don't hold your breath." He ambled over, and gave a cursory glance under the hood. "Anything could be wrong, and I wouldn't recognize it."

He backed off and nodded to Tava. "My advice to you, young lady, is to call a tow truck."

Tava, standing by helplessly, agreed. "Thank you anyway, Rance. This hasn't been my day. Sorry to have been such a bother."

He shrugged. "Don't worry about it."

He turned, his shoulders drooping, and shuffled back along the path to his dwelling. Tava watched Rance go, feeling pity for him because of his unfortunate circumstances.

"He was certainly snippety," Dottie said.

"We must have upset him," Tava said

"That's Rance." Aunt Kate chuckled. "He was just being his contrary self."

Tava sighed and felt frustrated from her lack of knowledge about motors. "I suppose there's nothing left to do, except call a tow truck." She took out her cell phone.

"Call Jim's Garage," Dottie said. "He comes into the bank a lot. He's a nice person."

"He's the one who repaired my tire." Tava said. "Do either of you know the number right off?"

They didn't.

"Why not call Shane and save a towing fee," Dottie suggested.

"You think Shane would mind?" Tava said.

Aunt Kate waved her hand. "The way he looked at you last evening, I think he'd love to come." "Do you think he'd know anything about car motors?" Tava asked.

Dottie shrugged. "You can always call the garage later."

"Okay." Tava agreed. She slammed down the hood, picked up her shoulder bag from the front seat, and locked the car. She punched in Shane's number from the business card in her purse on her cell phone.

Zack answered. Tava had suspected Zack of trying to run her down, and hesitated. She steadied herself to keep from hanging up. Zack promised to give Shane the message as soon as he returned.

"We'll wait for Shane at your house, Aunt Kate," Tava said. "There's no use standing around over here."

"Of course," Aunt Kate said. "It's a nice day to walk. I'm glad we wore our sneakers."

"If it were ten degrees warmer, it would be perfect." Dottie giggled, and swung her arms as she strolled along.

Pepper emerged from a clump of bushes and trotted along with them.

Suddenly Dottie stopped. "I just thought of something, Tava. Call Shane back. He may have come in and Zack may not have remembered to tell him."

Tava furrowed her brow, remembering her suspicion that Shane might be helping Hobe to get Cherohala. She hoped she was wrong. "You think he would resent dropping everything, and driving the ten miles out here to check on my car motor?"

"You said it was a good date," Dottie quipped. "I'd think he'd jump at the chance to get to see you again!"

"Yes, we had a lovely time." Tava hesitated. "But he didn't ask me out again exactly. He said he wanted to show me the lake area, but he didn't set a time."

"Well there you see, he's interested," Dottie said.

Tava hesitated.

"Whoop-de-do!" Dottie gestured with her hands. "So you don't have another date set. All the more reason you should ask him to come. Then he'll know how you feel about him."

"I suppose you're right. What do you think, Aunt Kate?" Tava asked.

"I think it would be a good idea. You would save a towing and repair bill."

Tava's pulse sped up at the thought of seeing Shane again. "I'll do it." She punched in his number.

"If he can come, invite him to stay for lunch," Aunt Kate said, as they neared her house. "I'll make my special chicken salad."

"Tell him Aunt Kate makes a delicious chicken salad," Dottie added.

Right off, Shane answered the phone.

"Zack gave me your message. I was about ready to call you. What can I do for you?"

Tava told him about her problem. "By the way were you out at Cherohala this morning?"

"Remember I'm not selling Cherohala any more. If I had known you were there, I might have dropped in." He sounded eager to look at the car motor, and promised to leave at once.

Tava waited for Shane on Aunt Kate's front porch. A tingling warmth spread over her when he turned the car into the drive a half an hour later. Shane strode up the walkway. Dressed in hunter green trousers, a pale green shirt, and an ivory colored half buttoned cardigan.

"Hi, Tava," he greeted, a smile plastered across his face. Tava hurried down the steps to meet him, her knees wobbling. "Thank you for coming. I'm sorry it had to be under these circumstances."

"What circumstances!" he teased, and reached out for her hand. He gently squeezed it. Tava trembled from the unexpected contact.

"You're shaking!" Shane appeared surprised. He withdrew his hand, and placed his arm around her shoulder.

"I feel ridiculous," she said, wishing she could control the trembling.

"Don't worry about it. Everyone has car trouble sometimes."

Tava giggled nervously. "You're right." She felt relieved he thought it was the car, and not his touch that caused her reaction.

He guided her to the passenger's side of the car, and opened the door. On the way to Cherohala she calmed down, and told him about the box that had disappeared.

"What!" Skepticism blanketed his face. "Don't expect me to believe a Cherohala ghost took the box."

They both laughed while Tava told him about the missing furniture, and the planned trip to see Mrs. Trowbridge.

"If Mrs. Trowbridge doesn't have it, or know the whereabouts of the furniture, call Elisa," he said. "She can check Jess's will. He may have written instruction about it."

"A great idea." she said.

"We men are indispensable."

"I believe that. You were kind enough to come out here."

"Think nothing of it." He shrugged. "I work hard to please is my motto."

"I like that motto."

"Good. I hope it's true. If it isn't, it should be. It will be my policy if I ever get my own realty company."

"You have dreams too."

"Don't we all? It can't be soon enough." He turned into Cherohala's drive and parked beside Tava's car. "I've got to get away from Zackery and Yates Realty."

"Really!" Tava gaped in surprise.

"I can't go into the situation now." They got out of the car.

Tava hurried to unlock the car door and raised the hood.

"I forgot to tell you, I'm not mechanical minded." He grinned in a teasing manner.

"Oh, no! Not you too."

"I probably would notice if something is out of place." He bent over. "Aha! I see a problem already. Look at this! The battery cable is disconnected." He pointed, reached down and fingered it.

Tava eased closer to see. "What caused it to come loose?"

"I have no idea." He spread out his hands. "Watch me as I reconnect it. If it happens again, you'll know what to do."

Tava stared. "Do you think someone did it on purpose or could it have come loose accidentally?"

"Is that a trick question?" He laughed, and slammed down the hood. "Why do you think someone did it on purpose?"

"Uh…" she stammered. "Too many things have happened to me since I've been here. She ticked them off with her fingers. "You can't call them all coincidences."

"Hmm. I see your reasoning. The flat tire is suspect and someone could have easily disconnected the battery cable. But who?"

She shook her head. "I have no idea."

"It's also hard to believe someone tried to run you down. If anything else happens, we'll have to hire a body guard." He laughed, and with his fist playfully tapped her shoulder. "Go ahead and see if your car starts."

Tava slipped inside the car and turned on the ignition. The motor purred right off. She gave a sigh of relief, her eyes twinkling with warmth for Shane. "Thank you! You brightened my day."

He waved. "Glad to help a lady in distress."

"I hope you haven't had lunch." She repeated Aunt Kate's invitation, and Dottie's opinion of the chicken salad.

"Your Aunt Kate is a good cook. Her reputation is well known."

"Is that a yes?"

He slapped his hands to his forehead. "I'm tied up for lunch. Tell Aunt Kate, I'm sorry, and will she invite me again." He leaned inside Tava's car, and gave her a swooping kiss on her brow.

Tava, taken aback by the gesture, felt a little frustrated. There was no way she could respond to his affection while seated inside the car.

Shane reached out to close her car door, but hesitated. "I just had a thought. The person who acquired Jess's furniture may have returned to pick up something else from the house. He saw the tin box, and took it."

"But my car was parked in the drive."

"People often park their cars here and walk down to the lake."

"That seems farfetched, but it might explain it," Tava said. He nodded toward the old house.

"Cherohala is getting to be a weird place for you, isn't it? Aren't you glad Hobe's taking it off your dad's hands?"

Tava's cheeks burned from anger. "No, I'm not!"

Right off she realized how she had sounded, and clapped a hand to her mouth. "I'm sorry. I didn't mean to jump at you."

"That's okay."

"I know Hobe desperately wants to buy Cherohala. My dad would have told me if he had agreed to Hobe's offer. If I have my way, Hobe will never own this place. I intend to buy it!"

Shane stared. "You do?"

"That's my dream."

"Now I understand your reaction to what I said. I hope your dream comes true."

"We'll have to get together and share our plans in detail," Tava said.

He shrugged. "I'm available."

Tava's heart sank. He hadn't responded with a time or place as she had hoped. "I'll be around for a few days."

"Good. I'll see you then." He closed her car door.

Tava whipped around his car, and waved to him as she sped away. She clung stubbornly to a thread of hope that he cared for her.

CHAPTER THIRTEEN

"I'm ready to leave anytime," Tava said after a leisurely meal of Aunt Kate's chicken salad on toast. She was anxious to be on the way to visit Mrs. Trowbridge.

"No argument from me." Dottie pushed back her chair.

"Let me grab my purse," Aunt Kate said.

"I'll drive," Tava volunteered, and walked toward the front door. "Point me in the right direction." Half an hour later they were parked in front of Mrs. Trowbridge's tiny white house.

Tava wondered how Mrs. Trowbridge had managed to get any large piece of furniture into such limited space. Aunt Kate shivered in the nippy spring afternoon, and pulled a pink cardigan around her shoulders tighter. She led the way along Mrs. Trowbridge's daffodil edged walkway.

Mrs. Trowbridge, a stout grandmotherly type with salt and pepper hair pulled back in a bun, met them at the door. She wore an undersized black sweater over a shapeless blue dress. "I'm so happy you all came to see me!" Her voice bubbled. She reached out and drew all three of them into her embrace. She released them and stared at Tava.

"Kate, you told me her name on the phone, but I can't remember now."

Tava quickly introduced herself.

Mrs. Trowbridge grabbed Tava's hand and enthusiastically pumped it, all the while smiling. Her eyes seemed to disappear in the folds of her cheeks. "Any kin of Jess's is welcome in my house."

"Thank you," Tava said.

"So you're Jess's niece."

"Great niece," Tava corrected.

"I'll declare, Tava, you're so pretty. Too bad you couldn't have come while Jess was living." She wagged her finger. "Of course, I'm not scolding you. I understand your situation. You lived too far away."

Tava nodded. "I'm sure it was my loss."

They followed Mrs. Trowbridge through the doorway, and into the sitting room. Mrs. Trowbridge repeated, "I'm so happy you-all came to see me. It's very lonely when you live by yourself."

Her words flowed out like torrents, as if she had so much to say, and not enough time to say it.

Tava glanced around the small room. There were no antiques. Veneered end tables sat on both sides of a sofa, covered in floral chintz. A tan swivel chair and a plaid colored recliner were spaced in front of a television set.

"Have a seat." Mrs. Trowbridge gestured with her hands. Aunt Kate eased down on the recliner, and Dottie chose the swivel chair. Tava backed up to the sofa.

Mrs. Trowbridge plopped down beside Tava, and asked, "What brought you here?"

"Cherohala," Tava smiled.

"She's thinking of buying it." Aunt Kate nodded.

"Well, I'll declare." Mrs. Trowbridge said. "I thought your dad would buy it."

"I hope to buy it from him," Tava said.

"Good for you." Mrs. Trowbridge leaned back and chuckled. "I'll be happy to see all of Jess's affairs settled. Of course, I don't know what you'd want with an old house like that! I've lived there, and believe me, it's in bad shape."

"Uh...." Tava started to explain.

Aunt Kate interrupted. "She knows what shape it's in. We've been over at the house all morning, looking through the rooms."

"You have!" Mrs. Trowbridge gaped. "I tried to straighten the place up after Jess went into the nursing home, but I guess it's all dusty by now."

"There's not much left to get dusty," Aunt Kate said. "Most of the furniture is gone."

"You don't say!" Mrs. Trowbridge appeared dumbfounded. "Who'd want that old stuff?"

"That old stuff is antique," Dottie said.

"Well, I'll declare." Mrs. Trowbridge's eyes widened. "I didn't know it was valuable!"

"Rance Bottoms said you might know what happened to it," Tava said.

"Rance said that?" A pained expression clouded her face. "You think I took it?"

Tava held up her hand. "I didn't mean to imply you took it. Jess had the right to give it to anyone he chose. I'm not trying to take it back. I just want to see it."

Mrs. Trowbridge's face softened into a smile. "Jess did give me three pieces. I'll be happy to show them to you."

Dottie winked at Aunt Kate, as if to say, "I told you so."

"Good, I'd like to see them," Tava said.

Mrs. Trowbridge arose from the sofa. "They're in my bedroom." She led the way into a small room, cramped with unmatched pieces of inexpensive furniture.

Tava, expecting to see a four-poster bed, or massive chest, was disappointed.

Mrs. Trowbridge removed a yellow-fringed scarf from an old fashioned pedal sewing machine, and asked, "Kate, do you remember sewing on one of these?"

"I sure do. In fact I preferred it over my electric one."

"And here's the crank-up record player." Mrs. Trowbridge rubbed her hand across the dark stained cabinet top, and opened it. "It still works. I've got a few old scratched records." Then she turned toward a well-worn unpainted cane-bottomed rocking chair. "This is the third piece, and the most used. I asked Jess for all these pieces. He didn't seem to want to part with them, but he left them for me in his will."

"I'm glad you got them," Aunt Kate said. "I guess he couldn't refuse, the way I waited on him those last few years."

"Jess was lucky to have you, I'm sure," Tava said.

"These were the only pieces of furniture I wanted from the house. I didn't really care for anything else," and she waved her hands around, "and where would I have put anything?"

"The dining room furniture and most of the bedroom pieces are gone," Aunt Kate said.

Mrs. Trowbridge shook her head. "I don't know what could have happened to the furniture. Unless Jess gave it away after he went into the nursing home."

"Or sold it," Dottie said.

"If Jess sold his furniture, he changed his mind completely." Aunt Kate said.

"I agree," Mrs. Trowbridge said.

"Do you think he sold it to pay his medical bills," Tava asked.

"Not if he left a tidy sum to his kinfolk," Mrs. Trowbridge said.

"Jess never confided in me about his finances," Aunt Kate said. "But, I'm sure he could pay his own way."

"Don't feel bad, Kate." Mrs. Trowbridge said. "He didn't confide in me either."

"Could the grandsons have taken the furniture?" Dottie asked.

Mrs. Trowbridge thought for a second. "I doubt it. They didn't know Jess had died until his attorney, Mr. Whitehead, notified them. I met the grandsons for the first time in Mr. Whitehead's office when Jess's will was read."

"Was there any mention of the furniture?" Tava asked.

"If there was, I didn't hear it. You could call the attorney and find out for sure."

"I heard the grandsons were upset over the will," Aunt Kate said.

Mrs. Trowbridge put her hand to he check, as if to recall something. "I don't know about that. One of the grandsons did ask if Jess was of sound mind when the will was drawn up. Mr. Whitehead assured him he was, and everything was proper and legal."

"It doesn't sound like the grandsons have any legal grounds for a law suit," Tava said.

"I think Jess did right by them, and they should be happy," Mrs. Trowbridge said. "He left them what was left of his savings."

"When did Jess make his will?" Tava asked.

"About a year before he went into the nursing home." Mrs. Trowbridge said. "I remember it well. Mr. Whitehead and this young lady lawyer came to Cherohala with all the necessary forms to fill out. I wanted to stay and listen, but Jess shooed me out of the room. I didn't know then he was leaving me those three pieces."

"Was the young lawyer, Elisa Rhodes?" Dottie asked.

"Yes. She's a smart person, and pretty too." Mrs. Trowbridge lowered her voice, as if speaking in confidence.

"I wonder if there's anything between her and that handsome young real estate salesman?" She was talking about Shane, Tava realized, and felt her face flush with jealousy. She stared at the floor. Aunt Kate glanced at Tava. "I wouldn't know."

"If there is, she has plenty of competition," Dottie said.

Mrs. Trowbridge led them back to the sitting room. "I can't get over the missing furniture." They resumed their seats.

"Why do you want to see Jess's old furniture, Tava?" Mrs. Trowbridge asked.

"I'd like to refurnish Cherohala with similar pieces."

"She wants to make Cherohala into a museum," Dottie added.

"A museum! I'll declare. That will take a lot of doing, but it's better than trying to live there."

"I don't know why Jess didn't mention the furniture to me, or to you, Mrs. Trowbridge!" Aunt Kate said.

"Just like him not to tell." Mrs. Trowbridge shook her head. "He was one tight-lipped man."

"Was there anyone he might have confided in?" Tava asked.

Mrs. Trowbridge chuckled. "I've wondered about that. I came home on weekends, until his condition worsened. Sometimes when I returned on Monday, I'd find the sitting room in a mess, as if he'd had company. When I teased him about it, he'd say, "I'm not too old for admirers!""

"Sometimes I went to see about him on weekends," Aunt Kate said.

"I don't think it was you, Kate. There were dirty glasses on the coffee table, and a stale smell of smoke."

"No, I don't smoke, and I wouldn't have left dirty glasses."

"I asked Jess about his guest again. He called me a meddling old woman who didn't respect his privacy." Mrs. Trowbridge laughed.

"Could it have been Rance?" Tava asked.

"Not likely. They didn't socialize. I asked Rance who had been visiting Jess on the weekends. He replied it was none of his business, nor mine."

"Rance can be crotchety at times," Aunt Kate said.

Mrs. Trowbridge spread her hands. "That's right. Rance seemed to carry a chip on his shoulder. Although he was a lot of help to Jess, he upset him. I think he did it once too often, because Jess left him out of the will."

"Did you ever find out who the visitor was?" Aunt Kate asked.

"No. I heard Jess on the phone one day talking to someone. He was so angry he was shaking. I thought I head him say Mr. Zackery, but I can't be sure. When I entered the room, he slammed down the phone and just glared at me."

"There's several Zackerys living around here,' Dottie said.

"Yes, I know," Mrs. Trowbridge conceded.

"Jess could have been upset at the idea of going into the nursing home," Aunt Kate said.

Mrs. Trowbridge nodded. "That's true! Who wouldn't be?"

Tava sat on the sofa, and tried to untangle the mysteries that seemed to grow. Would she ever be able to sort them all out? She puzzled over the situation of the missing furniture all the way back to Aunt Kate's house.

CHAPTER FOURTEEN

Tava watched a television news show in the living room with Aunt Kate and Dottie in the afternoon. Her mind was hung up on the missing antiques. She must call her dad and fill him in on the details. She arose from the chair, and hurried into the kitchen for privacy to make the call on her cell phone. There was no answer at his office or at home. She returned to the living room and glumly sank back down in a chair.

Dottie glanced up. "What's your problem, Tava?"

Tava told her.

"While you're waiting, why not take Mrs. Trowbridge's advice, and call Elisa at the Whitehead Law office. She could probably tell you right off if the furniture was mentioned in Jess's will."

Tava remembered Shane had suggested the same thing. She hesitated, dreading the contact with her rival, Elisa.

Dottie glanced at her watch. "The law office will close soon."

"Of course." Tava stood up. It was something she must do.

"Elisa is really a nice person," Dottie said. "You ought to get to know her better."

Tava nodded as she left the room to make the call. She punched in the number and asked for Elisa.

Elisa assured Tava there was no mention of any furniture in Jess's will other than what Mrs. Trowbridge had received. Then she said, "Your dad has the first option to buy Cherohala and its contents. That means whatever was left in the house."

Tava thanked her.

"Wait!" Elisa said. "Do you have a minute?"

"Sure."

"Shane told me about your interest in Cherohala and the furniture."

"Oh." Tava stiffened at the idea of Shane and Elisa together.

"Perhaps Jess gave the furniture to someone you'd never think about while he was in the nursing home," Elisa said. "I have a suggestion. Why don't you run an ad in the local paper inquiring about the antiques? Specify you only want to see them and explain the reason."

"That's a great idea!" Tava forgot momentarily their rivalry.

"There's only one paper in town and most people read it. If the person who has the furniture reads it, or hears about it, you'll probably get a phone call, or perhaps an invitation to their home."

"I'll do that the first thing in the morning," Tava said.

"That will be too late, unless you want it in next week's edition. The paper is a weekly."

"Oh. I should get it in today?'

"In the next few minutes. They'll want cash. You're not a local and their office will be closed by the time you get here. Why don't I do it for you?"

Tava was taken aback by Elisa's thoughtfulness. "Of course. You're very kind."

"Tell me what you want to say?" Tava rattled off the message, and promised to stop by Elisa's office the following day, and reimburse her.

"Why don't we get together for a sandwich at the Lunch Box," Elisa asked.

"That would be great," Tava said.

Elisa gushed. "I have some special news I'm dying to tell you."

"Really." Tava felt flattered on one hand that Elisa would want to share a confidence with her. On the other hand, she wondered why she had chosen her to hear it?

"Noon tomorrow?" Elisa asked.

"Sounds great," Tava agreed.

Would the special news be about Cherohala? Another thought leaped to mind. Was it Elisa and Shane's relationship? Could it be their engagement? A sense of uneasiness blanketed her. The phone in her hand shook as she said goodbye. Tava repeated Elisa's remarks to Aunt

Kate and Dottie, while other possibilities multiplied in her thoughts. They assured Tava it couldn't be anything major like an engagement. Their assurance relieved her anxiety somewhat.

Tava felt much better when her dad returned the phone call. Right off, she asked about his decision on Cherohala.

Her dad spouted, "Has someone struck oil on Cherohala? Hobe Yates has been bombarding me with phone calls. Each time his offer grows. I turned them all down. You can relax now. If the place is that valuable, I can't afford to let it slip through my fingers."

"Thank goodness!" Tava sighed.

Aunt Kate and Dottie looked up, their eyes filled with questioning stares.

Tava broke into a smile, and jerked her thumb up for their benefit.

"I'm thrilled, Dad. Now I want to buy it from you." Tava heard her dad gasp, followed by a moment of silence.

"Buy it from me!" He sounded surprised.

"Cherohala is already in the family and you're an only child."

"I know. It's not quite the same." She poured out her dreams for the old house.

"You sound as if you've fallen under Cherohala's spell."

"You can call it that, Dad." Tava giggled.

"If you want it that bad, I'll buy it and give it to you."

"That's sweet of you, but I know your business is struggling and you can't take on any more debt. I prefer to take out a loan for it – it'll give me an opportunity to start building my credit." She asked him to set a price, and told him how she would finance it.

"How about my option price?"

"I'll double it," she said, quickly calculating the money she'd saved up since childhood and the work she'd have to do to make the museum into a profitable establishment. Tours, possibly a bed-and-breakfast, the possibilities were endless. College will have to wait a few years while she got the mansion back into shape.

He agreed to fly down in two days if possible, and sign the necessary papers.

Tava hung up the phone. Tears of happiness brimmed over in her eyes. She danced about shouting, "I'm buying Cherohala! I'm buying Cherohala!"

Dottie clapped her hands. "We figured that out. It's good news for me too."

"I suppose the odds were stacked in my favor." Tava beamed, savoring her victory.

"This calls for some kind of celebration," Aunt Kate said and embraced Tava. "I'm so happy for you. I suppose I should be happy for myself. I'll have a new neighbor. Even if it is a museum."

They all laughed.

Tava told Dottie how much money she'd need to borrow.

"Cherohala is worth much more," Dottie said. "I'll talk to the loan officer when I go to work in the morning. I don't see any problem."

"I'm so excited," Tava said.

"I assume you have a good credit rating," Dottie said.

"Yes. I'll make a list of my credit references."

"It's getting to be time for supper," Aunt Kate said.

"I can't eat now," Tava said. "I need to call someone about my good fortune."

"Why don't you call Shane?" Dottie suggested.

"I wonder if he'll still be at work?" Tava wrinkled her nose.

"What does it matter?" Dottie said. "He has a cell phone. If he's with a customer this late, he'll let you know." Tava punched in Shane's number. After several rings and no answer, she gave up. She imagined he were eating with Elisa, but refused to dwell on it in her happiness. "I'll try him later."

"Tava, you understand the bank can't do anything about the loan until your dad gets here, and signs the necessary papers for Cherohala," Dottie said.

"I understand. Can't you get the wheels started?"

"I'll see what can be done," Dottie promised.

Aunt Kate's land phone rang, and she picked it up. "Who?" She frowned. "It's for you, Tava."

Tava wondered if the editor of the weekly paper was calling back, or was it Shane? She shuddered in wonder, and whispered, "Who is it?"

Aunt Kate shrugged. "He didn't give a name, and I don't recognize the voice."

Tava snatched the phone. "Hello," she said in the best cheery manner.

"Go back to where you came from!" A gruff voice crackled.

"Who is this?" Tava demanded.

"Go at once! For your own safety!" The phone line clicked, and the dial tone returned. Tava feeling numb, turned toward Aunt Kate and Dottie. She opened her mouth to speak, but no words came out.

"Who was that Tava?" Dottie asked.

"I don't know."

"You look ashen!" Aunt Kate said.

Tava shook her head, and repeated the phone message.

"Whoever it was must have disguised his voice."

Aunt Kate wagged her finger. "He didn't sound normal to me."

"Who could it have been, and why would he want me to leave?" Tava asked, alarmed.

"It could be anyone." Aunt Kate said.

Dottie arose, and pushed her chair back. "Remember you gave this phone number to the newspaper for the ad."

Tava bite her lip. "That's right. But the ad hadn't come out yet. Whoever it was knew Aunt Kate's number."

"Anyone can get my phone number. It's in the phone book," Aunt Kate said.

"It sounds like someone doesn't want you to buy Cherohala," Dottie said.

"Of course they don't. A threatening phone call won't stop me. I'm just as determined as ever." Tava trembled all over in fear.

CHAPTER FIFTEEN

Tava, visibly shaken over the anonymous phone call, felt wide-awake at 11'oclock. She almost forgot that Shane hadn't returned her call. Aunt Kate and Dottie appeared upset over the phone call also. But Dottie had to get some rest, so she could work the next day. Aunt Kate stayed up with Tava, although she appeared upset too. "I can't imagine what is going on around here," she said. "It's bound to be about the old tumble down house, Cherohala. What on earth does anyone see in it?"

"Is there something that you don't know about Cherohala?" Tava asked. "I've racked my brain, but I can't think of anything else." Aunt Kate said.

"And who would want to harm you!"

"I'd like to know too. Someone out there is trying to do that!" Tava said.

"We'll talk to Sheriff Greene tomorrow, Aunt Kate said.

"I wish I had a sleeping pill," Tava said.

Let's both have a warm cup of milk instead before we go to bed," Aunt Kate suggested.

After a warm cup of milk, Tava went upstairs to bed. After tossing and turning she dozed off. The next morning Dottie gave Tava a word of advice before she left for work. "Try not to let that awful phone call ruin your day, After all, Cherohala will be yours in no time."

"Until I sign on the dotted line, I'll worry." Tava said.

"You'll need to keep busy," Aunt Kate said. "It'll take your mind off of the call."

"I agree," Tava said, "If I don't concentrate on something else for the next few days, I'll go out of my mind. I'll begin by helping you clear the clutter from the table."

"Did you finish the sketch you were doing for me?" Aunt Kate asked.

"No…" Tava frowned, thinking about it. "I'm afraid I lost interest. I'll do another one for you."

After Tava helped Aunt Kate tidy up the kitchen, she punched in Shane's cell number, and immediately he answered. She blurted out the good news; she was buying Cherohala.

He congratulated her in a crisp and business like voice over a din of chatter in the background.

She realized at once she had called at an inconvenient time. He was probably with someone at breakfast. She wished him a good day, and hung up. In her haste to get off the phone, she thought it best not to mention the threatening and anonymous phone call. Should she call him later?

She hesitated, and thought better of it. Why worry him?

"Tava, what are your plans today?" Aunt Kate asked.

"I'll do another picture for you!" The scenic lake area in back of Cherohala came to mind. It would make a delightful backdrop for any sketch. The idea lightened Tava's mood, despite the nagging worry of the upsetting call.

Tava hurried upstairs, and changed into a blue striped blouse, jeans, and a beige windbreaker. She returned to the foyer with a tote bag, brimming over with art materials in one hand, and clutched her shoulder bag in the other. Slipping on her watch, she called out to Aunt Kate, "I'm leaving now."

Aunt Kate poked her head through the doorway. "Where are you off to?"

Tava told her. "It will probably take several hours, or most of the morning."

Aunt Kate wrinkled her forehead.

"The lake area! Aren't you afraid to go over there alone? Especially after that phone call!"

"I don't intend to let it ruin my day." Tava bristled with bravado, but felt weak-kneed.

"I can't let the phone call make a prisoner out of me. Whoever called won't know I'm there. I'll have my cell phone."

"I reckon you're right." Aunt Kate's voice lacked conviction. "Don't forget the lunch date with Elisa."

"Oops. I'm glad you reminded me." She bit her lip, and wished she could forget about it, except she had promised. "If I get a phone call about the furniture, don't give out my number. Just take the message?"

"Of course. Are you driving over there?"

"No. I'm walking. After those two happenings to my car at Cherohala, I'm not taking any more chances, until the place belongs to me."

Aunt Kate nodded. "Maybe a walk will be good for you. But do be careful. Should I come along?"

"I do better when I'm alone," Tava said. "Then what could you do standing over there by the lake?"

"You're right. I'm not even a fisherman," she said. "I'll take Pepper along," Tava said.

"Pepper wouldn't let you get out of his sight." Aunt Kate chuckled.

Tava, carrying her tote bag filled with painting supplies, and her shoulder bag tucked to her body, she walked briskly along the blacktopped road. She tried to minimize the worrisome phone call, but it hung on. Pepper trotted along beside her, which gave her a bit of courage.

THE SPELL OF CHEROHALA

The morning air was chilly, despite the sunlight that buttered the hilly landscape. Tava zipped up her windbreaker.

The highway seemed almost deserted. Only a few cars and pickups whizzed by. Tava assumed it was the time of morning; too late for workers, and too early for shoppers.

She focused on plans for Cherohala. Hobe popped into her thoughts. Surely he would know by now that Cherohala would be hers. She knew he desperately wanted the place, and wondered how would he react to the news? Always the perfect gentleman, he would surely offer congratulations. She smiled smugly to herself, feeling triumphant. At once the emotion shamed her.

Tava paused in Cherohala's drive, and stared at the old mansion. It seemed an aura emanating from the house beckoned her. She rubbed her eyes, and looked again. Her overactive imagination was working again. She viewed the old house in a different light, now that it was almost hers.

"Almost mine," she whispered to herself, and trembled slightly, reveling in her good fortune. She would drop out of school for a semester, and oversee the restoration of the house. It would be one big learning experience. Perhaps she'd get to know Shane better, even if he and Elisa became a

THE SPELL OF CHEROHALA

couple. She'd try to over come her attraction to
Shane by throwing herself into the restoration.

She glanced toward Rance's shack. The front
door stood ajar. He was nowhere in sight. Was
he's sleeping late or nearby? The presence of his
open door of his humble living quarters reassured
her that she was not entirely alone.

Cherohala's yard, ragged with weeds, and
wet with dew, dampened Tava's sneakers as she
tramped across it. She stamped her feet on the
graveled walkway. The lawn needed to be cut.
That would be the first chore on her list. Perhaps
she could hire Rance to mow it. Was there a
mower in the tool shed? She'd check that later.

"Come along, Pepper," Tava called. She felt
a bit more secure with the dog at her side. She
ambled down the lake trail, and ducked under a
dangling apple tree limb in the orchard. The
pathway needed to be cleared - another chore for
the list.

The soft lapping of the water against the
shore greeted her as she emerged into the
bottomland. Pepper darted into the thick rushes
that grew along the water's edge. Tava shaded
her eyes from the sun with her hand, and peered
about for a suitable place to sketch. A sandy spot
with a clump of cattails near the water appeared
ideal. She ambled over, dropping the tote and
shoulder bags down.

THE SPELL OF CHEROHALA

The cliffs, along side the lake waters, fascinated her. They had been created eons ago and stood like silent sentinels. According to Aunt Kate's story, Horace Henner had hidden the heirlooms at Click's Bluff, the tallest of the group.

Suppose the heirlooms had been recovered long ago by someone other than the Henner family? She strolled toward the legendary bluff for a closer look and glanced at her watch. Time was getting away from her. Pepper came out of the rushes, and followed.

The front of the precipice dropped sharply down, and its base was submerged in the lake waters. Its backside inclined gradually into the bottomland. Small to medium boulders clung precariously along its slope. Tava mused. The bluff appeared an unlikely hiding place. Could the chest have been buried at its bottom? If so, the chest would probably now be in the lakebed. The back part of the cliff appeared easy enough to scale. Perhaps Horace had found it too difficult to carry the chest that high. Had he hidden the treasure in crevice near the top? A chest or trunk could not have stood the ravages of nature that long.

Suddenly Tava had an overwhelming desire to climb the cliff. She hadn't scaled a cliff quite that high. But it didn't seem to be beyond her ability. It would be exhilarating. Perhaps it would take her mind off of the anonymous call. She would sketch Aunt Kate a picture later. She gingerly placed her sneakers into cracks and indentations of the rocky slope. She clambered partly up with childlike glee. She glanced down at Pepper, who eyed her with accompanying wagging tail.

"Come on, Pepper," she cajoled and giggled when he scrambled after her. Aunt Kate would never believe she had a climbing dog.

Tava wondered how high she could climb. What would she see from the summit? In a reckless mood she threaded her way upward. A sharp breeze whipped across her face. Near the top she paused to catch her breath. She propped her feet against a small rock, and took stock of her position. The pinnacle was only a few feet above her head. Should she dare climb higher? She glanced around. There didn't seem to be any evidence of a crevice or hiding place on the cliff. Suddenly her prop rock dislodged and she lost her footing. Slipping, she yelled, and grabbed onto a ledge. The rock thundered down the side of the slope, creating a miniature avalanche.

She clung to the outcropping, and stared below wide-eyed. Feeling giddy from the scare, she closed her eyes momentarily, and promised herself to be more careful.

After her fright subsided, she dared to look. A sapphire sky wrapped around her like a canopy, and the sun warmed her face. The panoramic view was breathtaking from her vantage point. She felt deliciously alive. In the distance bits and pieces of the ribbon-like highway were visible. In the opposite direction the lake waters glistened. What a gigantic setting for a landscape sketch. In her delight, she remembered what she had come to do, and reluctantly worked her way down.

In the descent she glanced about for Pepper. He was nowhere in sight. She chuckled. Perhaps he had already made his way down. By now, he was probably on the scent of some little animal nearby. She returned to the sandy spot she had chosen, and sank languidly on the ground. Sitting cross-legged, she wished she had a fluffy cushion.

What could she sketch? The area abounded in ideas; lake waters, cliffs, rushes and cattails. She chose the cattails as the focal point of the picture, and took out a pen and pad from the tote bag. Soon she became absorbed in her work, lulled by the sounds of the soft rippling water, rustling bushes, and the roar of an occasional vehicle speeding along the Ball Play road.

Tava glanced up, she had lost track of time, and checked her watch. She gasped. Where had the morning gone? It was almost time to stop. She eyed the sketch, and added a few more touches. She thought of Pepper. She hadn't heard the sharp sound of Pepper's familiar barking when he had treed some little animal. When pinpricks jabbed at her legs, she scrambled up, and hopped about. She chided herself for sitting too long in one position. Her creative mood had fallen to its lowest ebb. She promised herself she'd finish later.

The silence was shattered by a shrill scream. Was it a human voice or a man's cry? Another scream followed. They came from the direction of Cherohala, and sounded like cries of pain. Tava stood rigid, listening, but heard no more.

Who it could be, she wondered? Had it been Rance? There was only one way to find out. She snatched up her shoulder bag and raced up the trail. At the orchard she heard a racing car engine. By the time she reached the open spaces of Cherohala's yard, there was no car in sight. Had the car been in the driveway or on the highway?

Tava, out of breath, paused, and scanned the area. She saw no one and felt relieved. Had it been some kind of horseplay? Someone yelling from a moving car? Had she been alarmed over nothing?

She decided to return to the lake area, and pick up her tote bag. She hesitated with second thoughts. Perhaps Rance would have an answer, if he were nearby. She hurried toward his place. Near his shack she squinted at something crumpled on the ground, and realized it was a man. She gasped, and rushed toward him.

The man, all bloody, rolled over, and rose shakily to his feet.

She recognized his red plaid shirt, and sprinted toward him, yelling

"Rance!"

He stumbled into his shed like house and slammed the door, moments before Tava reached him.

Tava rapped on the door, yelling, "Rance! What happened to you?"

When he didn't answer, she banged on the door again. She waited a minute, and tried to open it. The door was locked. She yelled louder.

"This is Tava. Do you need a doctor?"

She heard only groans. Again, she pounded at the door. His voice crackling, he yelled, "Go away and leave me alone!"

"I'm not leaving until you open this door, and tell me what happened!"

She waited briefly, and added, "If you don't open the door, and tell me something, I'm calling 911 or the sheriff."

A few seconds later there was a stirring noise inside, and the door cracked a bit. A bent over Rance, his face bloodied and his eyes swollen almost shut, peered out.

Tava sucked in her breath. "You look terrible! What happened?" She rammed a foot between the door and the threshold.

"None of your business!" He tried to close the door. When he noticed her foot, he stopped.

Tava pushed against the door, trying to open it wider.

"You look like you need to go to the hospital emergency room!" Holding onto the door, he shook his head, "No! I'm not going anywhere! Go away and leave me alone!"

"Whoever did this to you shouldn't get away with it. Let me call the Sheriff."

"Please don't do that!" He opened the door wider. "You'll get me into more trouble. This is personal. You wouldn't understand. I'll take care of it in my own way."

"But Rance, you may be hurt worse than you think!"

"Go back to where you came from. Go now!" He sounded angry, and closed the door.

A sudden inexplicable chill came over Tava. She stood dazed. Rance had been the anonymous caller!

CHAPTER SIXTEEN

Tava turned away from Rance's door, her hands shaking. Why had he warned her? Was the call connected to his attack? What kind of person would assault him in such a despicable manner? Was he covering up for one of her distant relatives, angered over Cherohala going to an outsider? Had the person vented his wrath on Rance? Was she in danger? A spasm of fright swept over her.

She reasoned that no one could gain control of Cherohala by injuring her. It was a function of a court of law to transfer property. In her fright she raced back toward Aunt Kate's house. She took out her cell phone to call for help, but remembered Rance's request, and put the phone back in her shoulder bag. He had to be afraid of someone, and in fear didn't dare ask for help. She hoped Aunt Ruth would know what to do. She felt frustrated between a sense of pity for Rance, and a helplessness to do anything about it, as she hurried along. If only he had opened up to her. Perhaps together they could have dealt rationally with the situation.

Tava, breathing rapidly, burst into Aunt Kate's sitting room.

Aunt Kate was talking on the phone. She jotted something on a notepad, and turned to Tava, gaping. "What's wrong?"

Tava related Rance's condition, and who the anonymous caller had been.

Aunt Kate stared aghast momentarily. She snatched up the phone.

"I'm calling an ambulance for Rance, and then the sheriff."

Tava held up her hand. "No! Rance refuses to go to the hospital, and begged me not to call the Sheriff. He's afraid of someone, and wants to deal with him in his own way."

"Take matters into his own hands!" Aunt Kate pursed her lips. "No good can come from that."

Tava nodded. "I agree."

"What about your safety, Tava? Maybe you should call the Sheriff."

"You're right. If I do, I'll have to implicate Rance." Tava wavered. "Surely no one can gain anything by harming me. Besides, Rance said it was personal."

Aunt Kate's eyes narrowed. "Rance is protecting someone."

"Who could it be?"

"I don't know."

Tava repeated Hobe's remarks about a distant cousin.

"That's hard to swallow." Aunt Kate shook her head. The only relatives I know, besides you, your dad, Dottie, and Shane, are Jess's grandsons."

"Are you sure?" Tava asked.

Aunt Kate put her hands on her hips. "Good heavens! You don't suspect a relative would be the cause of all this mischief, do you!" Tava shrugged.

"Can you think of anyone who would benefit from Cherohala?"

"Oh, my!" Aunt Kate slapped her hands to her face. "I just thought of something dreadful. The grandsons would profit more if someone else bought Cherohala."

"That's right. Cherohala would sell for much more, and the money would probably go to them."

"Maybe you need a lawyer, Tava."

"I'll talk to Elisa at lunch."

"That reminds me. Elisa called." Aunt Kate glanced at the note pad in her hand. "She's free at noon for lunch with you. She wants you to call before you leave."

"Oops!" Tava said, glancing at her watch. "I'm late already."

"Wait. There's more. Shane called and apologized for being abrupt on the phone. He'll call later and explain." Aunt Kate smiled knowingly.

Tava's face lit up. "Really!" She had a lot to tell him.

"There were two calls about your ad in the newspaper."

Tava gaped. "They have the furniture!"

"I'm afraid not. But they have some antique furniture they will sell you."

"Oh."

"The antiques might just be the pieces you'll need to refurnish Cherohala."

"That's an idea." Tava snapped her fingers. "I almost forgot. I left my tote bag with the art materials at the lake. I'll drive over and for them, and check on Rance once more."

"I'll come with you. You shouldn't be alone."

"I'll be okay. Whoever beat up Rance is gone. Could you call Elisa for me? Tell her I'm running thirty minutes late."

"All right. Take Pepper with you."

"Didn't Pepper come home?"

"I haven't seen him. I thought he went with you."

"He did. But he wandered off." She hesitated about mentioning Pepper climbing the slope. It wasn't the time.

"He'll turn up," Aunt Kate said. "He always does."

"I'll be back shortly to dress for lunch."

With the wave of her hand, she rushed out the door.

Tava parked in Cherohala's drive and locked the car. She scanned the area around Rance's place. She saw no one and his door was closed. She'd pick up the tote bag first, and then check on him. At the sound of a motor vehicle she glanced toward the highway, and expected to see a car or truck come into view. When she didn't, she assumed it had turned off someplace nearby. Aware of the time, she rushed down the trail.

The unfinished "Cattail sketch" lay on the ground where she had left it. She stared at it critically, and decided it was satisfactory. It would be a snap to finish. Slipping it inside the sketching tablet, she dropped it into the tote bag. Pepper came to mind. She called his name several times. When he didn't appear, she decided there wasn't time to bother. Aunt Kate had said he'd turn up. Picking up the tote bag, she heard a faint whine, and paused to listen. The whine grew louder, and came from the direction of the bluff. It sounded like an animal's cry of pain.

Was it Pepper? What was he doing on the cliff? She sucked in her breath. The small avalanche of rocks! Had it trapped him! She threw aside her shoulder bag and tote. Racing to the cliffs, her breath came in spurts. She called Pepper's name at the top of her voice, until she reached the base of Click's Bluff, and stared up. A yelp came from above, and she knew it was Pepper, although he was hidden from view. An image of a trapped Pepper, torn and bleeding came to mind. It was all her fault. What would

Aunt Kate think of her irresponsible behavior in coaxing Pepper up the slope? Guilt lay heavy on her, making her determined to find him.

Tava left her phone in the shoulder bag, along with the tote bag under a cattail clump, and clamored up the rocky slope again. She inched her way toward Pepper's muffled cries. She paused at a scrabbling noise near a rock pile, and crouched down, searching for him. His black button of a nose poked through a space in the rocks.

"Pepper! " Tava cried joyfully. She gently punched his nose with her finger.

"It's all right, Pepper. I'll get you out."

She clawed frantically at the stony rubble, trying to dislodge the smallest boulder that pinned in Pepper. After several futile attempts, broken nails, and bleeding fingers, she stopped. Wiping beads of perspiration from her forehead, she assessed the situation. A stout stick for a lever was needed. She glanced about. Not seeing anything she could use, she tried again to move the rocks with her hands by pushing and shifting. Pepper dug furiously from his position against the seemingly immovable stones. Tava held out her hands, sighed, and gave up. She needed help to free Pepper. At that moment Pepper broke through, and bounded out of his rocky prison. A fur ball of motion, he twirled around Tava's ankles in his newfound freedom.

Tava encircled him in her arms, holding him still for a moment, while she ran her fingers over his furry body for possible injuries. He licked her face and hands.

"Thank goodness you seem all right, Pepper." Relieved, she let him go.

He sniffed among the rocks that had held him prisoner.

Tava, limp from the ordeal, leaned against the side of the slope and rested. She smiled, watching Pepper like an indulgent mother. Suddenly aware of the time, she stared at her watch and gasped. It was half past noon. She needed to call Elisa, but no phone. Already late for the lunch date, she'd call after she climbed down. She had to check on Rance also.

"Let's go Pepper." She began the descent with a sense of urgency.

When she realized he wasn't with her, she became irritated, and yelled. "Pepper! Where are you?"

He stuck his head from behind a boulder higher up. He had climbed up instead of down.

"Oh, no, Pepper!" Tava scolded, thinking of another delay. Dogs surely don't become disoriented, she thought. Impatiently, she scrambled back up and scolded, "I suppose I'll have to lead you down by your collar!"

When she reached the spot, Pepper was gone. Upset, and in tears, she peered behind the rock. Pepper was half way inside a cleft in the bluff. His hind legs and tail stuck out.

"Pepper! Don't you dare go in there!" she screamed. Her words, in vain, echoed down the slope. Pepper disappeared before her eyes. Her heartbeat jarred her chest. She noticed the aperture covered

By tilting slabs of stone where Pepper had entered, and realized it was possibly wide enough for a person to slip through, if they stooped. She stared inside at a cave-like recess, and stared open-mouthed. Was Pepper in danger? She blindly ventured through the opening. A thin stream of light filtered through an overhead fissure, and created a shady passageway. Her eyes adjusted, and she saw Pepper sniffing up ahead.

"Pepper, come back!" she pleaded, imagining horrors ahead.

He ignored her, and kept going.

Tava hesitated. What should she do? Go after him, or leave him to his own folly? A feeling of responsibility kicked in, and she trailed after him. Elisa would have to give up on her. The cave appeared tame enough. She held onto the rocky wall, and warily followed after Pepper. The cave ended in a circular area. Awe struck, she gazed around. Something crackled under her feet. She shrieked, and jumped aside. Pepper dashed over, sniffed, and gave a low growl.

Tava squinted down at small bones and feathers strewn over the rock floor. She shuddered. The cave was a den for animals. An unusual rock at the back of the area reminded Tava of a stone bench. Rectangular in shape, it appeared to be about two feet long, and half as wide. She approached it, and marveled that the elements had created such a perfectly shaped stone inside a cave.

Pepper dashed against her legs, almost tripping her, on his way toward unusual stone. He sniffed and pawed at it. In the dim light Tava stared at the rock's patina. Could it be moss? She hunkered down beside it, and scratched its surface. Made of wood, and pitted with greenish mold, it was encircled with corroded metal bands. Suddenly she sucked in her breath. It was a chest!

"The hidden heirlooms!" she shouted, leaping up and down. Her heart raced in excitement. Had she discovered the legendary hidden treasure! Pepper eyed her, and gave a weak bark.

When Tava's exhilaration subsided, she kneeled again at the chest, and tried to open it with her sore fingers. She quickly realized it would take a tool to pry it open. Time had securely sealed it. What could be inside? Her fantasy ran wild. Was this where Horace had hidden the Henner valuables? Were the Henners' heirlooms valuable? To whom did the chest belong? Or was it finders' keepers?

She scooped up the chest in her arms. Despite its weight, she could lift it, but it would take stronger arms than hers to carry it down the cliff. She lowered the chest back into its spot.

Who could help her? Rance wasn't able. Shane came to mind. The idea of sharing the discovery with him brought a quickness to her chest. She envisioned the expression on his handsome face, when he heard the news. She chuckled in happiness, and started to call him, until she remembered again, she didn't have the cell phone. She realized she had to go for help.

"Stay, Pepper," she gestured with her hands, and wondered if he understood. Pepper wagged his tail, sidled over and lay down in front of the chest, as if he knew what it was all about and groped her way out of the cave. With a toss of her head, she reasoned the chest had been safe for over a century. Surely another hour or two wouldn't matter.

CHAPTER SEVENTEEN

Tava emerged from the cave, swung around the boulder near the entrance, and began the slow descent down the slope. Her thoughts were on the treasure chest, and her spirits soared. A feisty breeze skipped off the placid waters, and tangled her hair. The afternoon sun warmed her face.

About half way down, she paused, and glanced unconsciously toward the bottomland. A man, walking briskly and swinging his arms, came into view. He wore a white shirt, and blue trousers with a gray jacket slung across his shoulder. He glanced from left to right, as if he were searching for someone. He looked familiar. Seconds later when he came nearer, she recognized Hobe.

She puzzled. Why had he come? Who was he looking for? Had Dottie and Shane failed to tell him the news about Cherohala?

It was good that he had come, whatever his reason. She'd ask him for help, instead of making the arduous trip down the slope to call Shane.

"Hobe!' she yelled as he drew closer, and puzzled over his disheveled appearance. He paused, gazed up, and appeared startled.

She waved her arms wildly. "I'm on the cliff, Hobe!"

He cupped his hands over his eyes, turned toward the cliff, and squinted upward. When he saw her, he gaped. "Tava!"

"Are you looking for me?"

"Yeah. I saw your car, and knew you were around someplace."

"You found me." Had he come to make another offer for Cherohala?

"What are you doing up there, Tava?"

"It's a great story, Hobe. It should make the news."

"Well, I'm all ears."

"I'm dying to tell, but right now, I need help. Can you climb up here?"

"Climb up there!" A baffled expression crossed his face. "What for?"

"I found a chest, and I need help with it!"

"What!" There was disbelief in his voice.

"The treasure chest! You know. The Henner heirlooms.'

"That old legend! Are you putting me on?"

"No. I'm serious."

He shrugged, and waved his hands in a skeptical way. "You found a

Chest up there on the cliff!"

"That's right." She twisted around and pointed. "In a cave behind a boulder."

He cocked his head hesitantly as if weighing the validity of the story.

"I'll have to see to believe it."

"I know. Come on up."

"I'm not sure I can climb up there!"

"It's not as difficult as it looks. There are toe holds, and plenty of ledges to grasp onto."

He stood as if he were mulling it over, and stared up and down the cliff.

"I might give it a try. Won't we need a rope to bring the chest down?"

"A rope would be good. The chest isn't large, but it's cumbersome, and has no handholds."

He rubbed his forehead. "I saw a rope in the tool shed at the old house. I'll go and get it." He flung his jacket on a rock, and hurried back the way he came.

Tava watched him disappear in the distance, and eased down on a stone shelf to wait. In her euphoria, unselfishness abounded. Hobe could choose any item from the chest for his help, if it were left up to her. Soon Hobe returned with an old discolored rope coiled around his shoulder. At the foot of the cliff, he stared up.

After a moment of hesitation, he said, "I may be clumsy, but here I come."

"Take your time, Hobe, and work your way up. You can do it," she said encouragingly.

He struggled slowly upward, slipping, sliding, and uttering obscenities.

By the time he reached Tava on the cliff ledge, he was winded and perspiring. He mopped his brow with a white handkerchief, scowled at her, and said in a hostile voice, "Tava, this had better be good!"

She flinched at his words, but shrugged it off, thinking he was not in good physical shape for the strenuous climb.

"There's no doubt in my mind about the chest. Of course, I don't know what's inside."

He shoved the damp balled up handkerchief back into his pants' pocket.

She noticed dark splotches, resembling blood, scattered across the front of his shirt. "Oh, I'm sorry. It looks like you cut your hands on the climb. There's blood on your shirt."

"What!" His face flushed. He held up his hands, and stared. His right hand appeared bruised and swollen. "I don't see any blood," He quickly put his hands down.

"You probably wiped it on your shirt," she said.

He peered down at his shirt. "Oh, that?" He shrugged. "Oh. A nosebleed. A problem of mine."

Tava shrugged. "Sorry."

She accepted the explanation, and turned to lead the way up the cliff. She knew a nosebleed would account for his untidiness, but why were his hands bruised? The question churned in her thinking. When a bloody Rance came to mind, the back of her neck tingled. Had Hobe assaulted Rance? Had she stumbled into a nasty feud? At the thought of Rance's warning, she caught her breath, and paused. Cherohala must be involved! She glanced quickly over her shoulder at Hobe, hoping for some sign that her suspicion was groundless.

"Hey!" he yelled. "What's the hold up?"

"Aren't you tired?"

"What makes you think that?"

"Your appearance!"

"Let's get it over with," he said.

Tava held onto a ledge, and pulled herself up. Should she openly accuse him? She didn't fear him on the slope. Her agility gave her the edge. But if she were wrong, she'd make a fool of herself, and complicate getting the chest down. Despite feeling apprehensive, she continued the climb.

"How did you find the cave?" he asked pleasantly.

Tava lightened up. Perhaps she had misjudged him.

"Actually Pepper found the cave opening." She related the events.

He chuckled. "I can't imagine a dog on this cliff."

She did not explain how Pepper got up there. A few minutes later she reached the boulder that had concealed the cave opening, and waited patiently for a panting Hobe to join her.

"Are we close?" he asked, breathing rapidly.

"It's behind this rock." She pointed, and swung around to the mouth of the cave.

Hobe stared, open-mouthed. "No wonder it was never found!"

"Are you ready to go in?"

He nodded. Tava slipped through the opening.

Hobe ducked his head, and followed in a stooped position. "It's scary in here."

"You'll be able to see as soon as your eyes adjust." Tava once more held onto the rock wall, and made her way through the stony corridor to the spot of the find. She waved her hand. "Can you see the chest over there?"

Hobe squinted. "I see something."

Pepper leaped up when Hobe neared. He bared his teeth, raised his hackles, and snarled.

"Stop that dog!" Hobe ordered and jumped behind Tava. "He'll attack me!"

Tava shouted at Pepper, surprised at his ferociousness. Pepper did not stop.

Tava grabbed his collar from behind, and spoke calmly to him. "It's all right Pepper." She steered him to one side a few feet away, and stroked his back. "Lie down, Pepper."

Pepper, shaking all over, lay down reluctantly, his eyes fixed on Hobe.

"Whee," Hobe sighed. "He's one vicious dog."

"I don't know what's got into him," Tava said, "I suppose he's being protective of me."

"Do you think it's safe now for me to look at the chest?'

"I think so. Pepper seems to have calmed down." Tava led the way and kneeled beside it.

Hobe crouched down near the chest, and dropped the rope from his shoulder. He ran his fingers over the chest, and brushed his hand across the top, as if in doubt.

"No question about it, this is an old chest. It had to be hidden for some reason. How do you know it's the Henner heirlooms?"

Tava shrugged. "I can't be sure. It does fit the legend, and this is Click's Bluff where it was supposedly hidden."

"There's only one way to find out." Hobe took out a pocketknife, and opened the largest blade. He jabbed and scraped at the corroded edges of the lid without making any progress. In an outburst of temper, he flung the knife aside, and banged on the chest with both fists.

Pepper growled again. Tava, surprised at Hobe's childish display of anger, stared. An uneasy feeling gripped her, and she stood up.

"Ouch!" He shook his right hand, and drew back. He glanced sheepishly at Tava. "Okay. I'll take your word for it." He arose, still stooped.

"I never believed the tale about the heirlooms. But it could be true. Of course, the real treasures are the land, the lake waters, and their many possibilities."

Tava nodded in agreement, and asked, "Did Shane or Dottie tell you about my good news?"

"Yes, I heard." He grimaced and glanced down. "Good news for you. Bad news for me."

CHAPTER EIGHTEEN

Tava puzzled. Why had Hobe come looking for her? Was he going to make another offer for Cherohala? When Rance came to mind, a feeling of Impending danger spread over her. She stepped backward with no intention of becoming another victim. She'd watch his every move. Then there was her ally, Pepper.

Hobe nudged the chest with his foot. "What type of heirlooms are supposed to be in here?"

"I don't know. I'd guess gold coins, silver utensils, and jewelry. Stuff that was valuable about that time."

"What about pistols and swords?"

Tava raised her shoulders. "I suppose they would have wanted to keep their weapons at home for protection."

"Yeah, you're right." He wagged a finger. "Now I remember! There was supposed to be a list somewhere in a tin box. I thought it was nonsense."

Tava gaped. "What tin box are you talking about?"

"Uh…" He shrugged. "It must have been something Rance found."

Tava's face burned.

"Rance stole the tin box from Cherohala!"

Hobe shrugged as if he held contempt for the matter.

"How would I know where he got it?"

Tava threw back her shoulders, outraged Rance had stolen the tin box from the bottom of the stairs.

"He came in the old house while Aunt Kate, Dottie and I were there, and took the tin box. He lied about it!"

"Right. Rance can't be trusted." Hobe bent over, picked up the chest, weighing it in his arms.

"Not too heavy." He eased it back down. He took out his pocketknife, opened it, and cut several lengths of rope. He tied the pieces together and made a basket for the chest.

"When the chest is opened, I think you should get your pick of anything inside for carrying it down," she offered.

Hobe chuckled in a mocking sort of way. "Finders keepers, uh! How generous can you get?"

Tava realized his rebuff. "I thought you'd like something for your help. I couldn't ask Rance. Someone beat him up." She quickly put a hand over her mouth. She had a feeling she had said the wrong thing, and that Hobe was involved. She felt vulnerable.

"Did he tell you who beat him up?" Hobe's eyes narrowed as he stared at her, and waited for an answer. She shook her head, despite her suspicions, and told the truth. "He wouldn't tell me."

"But you suspect who did it!" Tava stared speechless, not sure how to respond.

"You've been playing cat and mouse with me, haven't you?" Hobe said, asking about the blood on my shirt. You think you're superior, don't you?"

Tava shook head. "I certainty don't!"

"I was the one who beat up Rance. He deserved every lick. You said he was a thief and a liar!"

She held out her hands. "Yes, I suspected you did it. But I don't want to get involved in your personal affairs."

"Personal!" He snorted contemptuously. "You're right in the middle!"

A shiver of fear ran down her spine. "I don't know what you're talking about!"

"Are you that naïve, or just playing dumb?" He stared at her. "You're bound to know by now it's Cherohala."

"Yes, but I don't know the particulars."

Hobe's face appeared contorted in the dim light.

"You and your ridiculous dream! You think you can turn a ramshackle old house into a museum? Why? To hold onto the past! The future is where it is! Why can't you understand that? There's a big demand for all types of water recreation since the dam was built."

He waved. "At the base of this cliff is a perfect place for a marina. There's plenty of land around the old house for rental cabins."

Tava stiffened in anger at his tirade, and her voice quivered with indignation. "Then it was no accident you put Cherohala up for sale before my dad's option ran out!"

"Right. I was testing the market. Why did your dad wait until the last minute? He wasn't interested. It was you!" He glared at her. "I knew Cherohala wouldn't sell at that price. I intended to lower it, and buy it myself."

She jabbed the air with her finger. Her eyes blazed, and her cheeks reddened. "You and Rance were behind all those things that happened to me! You were trying to scare me away. You didn't succeed!"

Hobe whacked off two more lengths of rope.

"Rance was responsible for most of what happened to you."

"Acting on your orders, I suppose," Tava quipped.

He shrugged.

"Now I know who almost ran me down," she said. "It wasn't Mr. Zackery. You were driving his car, weren't you?"

"Too bad it didn't scare you away." He continued talking as if she weren't there. "All this could have been avoided if Jess Henner hadn't been so pigheaded. I made him several great offers for Cherohala before he went into the nursing home. He laughed in my face. Kept repeating the place's heritage, like the house was alive. What good is heritage to a dying man?"

Tava thought of Shane. She caught her breath. Surely he wasn't mixed up in the conspiracy. She needed to know, and asked, "Who else was in on this scheme?"

"Who else! Oh, I see. You want to know about the fair-haired Shane, who you've fallen for! Why should I tell?"

Tava reasoned that Hobe would have gloated if Shane had been involved, and felt relieved somewhat.

"Greed was your motive. What was Rance's?"

"You don't know?"

"No."

"His great, great grandmother. After the War Between the States was disinherited from her share of the place, because she married a man who was suspected of having mixed blood. The final slap came when Jess left Rance out of the will, after he helped him for a long time. That's the kind of people the Henners were! You want to preserve all that! Rance has no home. I promised him he could stay on if he worked for me."

"Now I understand." She recalled Lavonia's letter in the attic, and Aunt Kate's explanation why Lavonia was denied her share. Rance was her distant cousin. "Why did you beat him up?"

"He backed out of our bargain, and I lost my temper. I have trouble controlling it. That's why I'm in this little backwater town."

"Why did you come looking for me, I had nothing to do with it!"

"I thought Rance told you who beat him up." He screwed up his face. "Let's say the chest saved your day."

Tava realized what he might do to her, now that she knew everything.

She waved her hand. "Take the chest and leave, Hobe. The secret will be between us."

"How big hearted of you! You think I'm that dumb?" He stood between Tava and the exit, his legs apart, scowling defiantly.

"Of course not." As much as she wanted the chest, she knew her safety came first. "I'm getting Cherohala. You should get something. Take the chest," she urged, and stepped backward, tripping over Pepper.

Pepper leaped up growing, and made a dive for Hobe.

Hobe held out his knife. "Stop that dog, or I will!"

Tava grabbed Pepper's collar. Trying to calm him down, she led him behind the chest, away from Hobe. He continued to growl, and eye Hobe. Hobe lunged at Tava, grabbing her by the arm, and pinned his left forearm around her neck. She tried to jerk free.

"What do you think you're doing?"

"I'm going to tie you up. Stop struggling, or you'll get hurt." He pressed the knife blade into her back.

"I said you can have the chest!"

"You'd beat me down the cliff, wouldn't you? I'd be arrested! Now put your hands behind your back."

Tava hesitated, trying to think what she should do. Could she escape with Pepper's help? She felt the knife blade dig deeper in her back, and quickly obeyed.

Hobe held the knife between his teeth, and bound her wrists with a strand of rope. "You're getting off easy."

Tava wondered if he would have done worse if he hadn't feared Pepper.

He ordered her to sit down on the stone floor, and tied her ankles together. Tava gasped when he yanked out his handkerchief, knowing he was going to gag her! Pepper gave a low guttural growl, his eyes riveted on Hobe.

"If you gag me, I can't control Pepper."

Hobe hesitated, and glanced toward the dog. "All right, but you'd better control that mongrel!" He stuffed the handkerchief back into his pocket.

"Why are you doing this, Hobe? You're throwing away a bright future in this community."

"I have no future here now, thanks to you." He lifted up the chest, slung it across his back, and adjusted the rope.

"If no one finds me, I'll die up here. Then you'll b a murderer."

Pepper continued to growl.

"Don't worry. That mongrel will save you." He turned to go, and glanced back. "Remember if that dog comes for me, you could be here all alone, and forever."

Tava heeded his sobering warning, and tried to control Pepper by her voice. When he disappeared from sight, she felt relieved, but more aware of her uncomfortable position and the rope that cut her skin. Pepper barked a few more times, before he trotted over to Tava. Trembling all over, he nestled down beside her.

She had never felt so helpless and miserable in her life. It was hard to believe this had happened to her. She glanced at Pepper, and felt thankful he was there.

CHAPTER NINETEEN

Tava, in a state of agitation, rocked back and forth in her cave prison. She assumed Hobe had gotten off the cliff by now. He must not escape. She had to free herself quickly, and report him to the Sheriff. It was important that the chest be recovered for the museum.

She stared at Pepper, who was biting at a flea on his leg. Could he help her?

"Pepper, go home!" She vigorously shook her head. "Go home and get Aunt Kate!"

Pepper jumped up, gave a short bark, and wagged his tail as if he understood. She repeated the command. Pepper gave another quick bark. With his nose to the cave floor, he sniffed, as if he were on the scent of a quarry, and dashed into the passage. Tava smiled as she watched Pepper dash out. She realized he was tracking Hobe, who would probably be in the bottomland or on the trail, and headed toward his car. Her flicker of hope turned to agony. What would Pepper do at the end of the trail? Would he go home, or become distracted by some little animal, and forget about her? What then?

She and Hobe were the only ones who knew about the cave. If Pepper didn't lead someone back, she could be there forever. She imagined someone scaling the cliff in the next century, and by chance finding the cave. Perhaps the person would stumble on her bones. The thought made her shudder.

The feeling of doom enraged her. Determined not to give up, she twisted her hands, moved her ankles back and forth to loosen the knots. After thrashing and squirming, the bonds bit into her wrists and ankles as tightly as ever. Damp with perspiration, she decided there had to be an easier way. She lost track of time. Had she been there an hour or longer? She wished she could see her wrist watch. Aunt Kate would be consumed with worry, especially when Pepper returned alone. She had promised her she'd return shortly. Would Aunt Kate send someone to the area to look for her? Or would she call the Sheriff? If someone came searching, they'd see her tote and shoulder bag. Surely it would be only a matter of time.

She had to yell. No one would know she was inside the cave, unless she made her presence known. She had heard Pepper's cries from the cliff.

"Help!" she yelled as loud as possible. The sound of her voice echoed through the cavern. She yelled until her voice became hoarse, and her throat scratchy. She rested her voice, but would yell again later. She continued to struggled against her wrist rope. Had the bonds loosened a bit? She decided they were as tight as ever.

She was distracted by a soft padding noise, and glanced up. She listened intently in the stillness of the cave. Pepper sallied forth, wagging his tail.

"You silly dog! You came back." She grinned, despite the graveness of the situation. His presence buoyed her up. "I told you to go home!"

Pepper trotted over to her, and licked her face, as if he had been gone all day.

Tava turned her head away from him. "You've got to go home, Pepper!"

He whined and circled around as if he were going to lie down. Instead he sniffed at her ankle fetters.

"Go home!" Tava yelled. "Bring someone back."

Pepper stared at Tava with his sorrowful eyes. Tava, frustrated at her failure to communicate with Pepper, drew her knees up, and kicked at him.

"Go home!" It took several tries at scolding before he reacted.

He turned slowly, tucked his tail between his legs and trotted out of the cave. This was the second time he had left, she thought, and felt the odds were stacked against his leading someone back.

She had to free herself, but how? Tied up in the uncomfortable position, she eased over on her side, and rested her head on the stone floor. Closing her eyes briefly, she drifted into a troubled sleep.

When she opened her eyes she was horrified. Darkness filled the cave, and blended in with the spooky silence. Had she slept all afternoon? She sat up. Her arms and legs tingled with pins and needles. Was she alone in the cave? Or was she sharing it with nocturnal animals that might attack? Could a slimy, slithering creature be only a few feet away? Her imagination ran amuck, and she broke into a cold sweat. At the same time her teeth started to chatter. She stared into the blackness, trying to discern any movement and listened for sounds of another presence. Not seeing or hearing anything, she breathed easier.

Disoriented, she tried to gain her bearing. Was the cave wall behind her? She scooted backward on her bottom, until she bumped into a stony edge. An idea grabbed her. Would the edge be sharp enough to cut the ropes? Why hadn't she thought of it sooner? She squirmed until she found the right position to rub her wrist bond against the stone wall. It was a slow and tedious process, but she had nothing else to do. At times she scraped her sore hands. Beads of perspiration trickled down her forehead. When she felt a strand of the rope give, she knew the ordeal was almost over. Finally her hands were free.

"Oh my gosh!" she cried and untied her ankle. Trembling, she stood up, holding onto the wall to grope her way slowly out of the cave. Outside a bright moon shone through the treetops and cast dappled patches on the side of the cliff. Below the ghostly bottomland pitched away to nothingness, and the lake waters lapped gently in their eternal rhythm. Tava breathed in the fresh air, and gazed about, hoping to see lights from a search party. There were none. Had they given up on her?

Climbing down the bluff in the moonlight appeared almost ordinary after escaping from the cave. She eased one foot down after the other, and slowly descended the side of the slope. When her feet touched ground, it seemed like she had been clinging to the side of the cliff forever. She wobbled a few steps, until her legs returned to normal. In her haste to return she had no thought of her tote or shoulder bag on the sandy beach.

She raced across the bottomland, and up the trail. Hobe must be apprehended as soon as possible. She must call Aunt Kate, and remembered her cell phone was inside her bag, and her car keys. Turning around, she went back for her belongings. Surprisingly they were still there. She took the phone out of her bag, and dialed Aunt Kate's number. There was no answer. After several tries she gave up, assuming Aunt Kate wasn't home. Perhaps she was out with a search party?

Shadows hung like curtains as she raced up the thicketed path. Her breath came in spurts. She couldn't run fast enough. When she broke into the clearing, and saw Cherohala all aglow from the beams of car lights, she choked up. They were searching for her around the old house, and near her car. Several people huddled together outside on the lawn. Soon she recognized Aunt Kate, Dottie, Shane, Elisa, Mr. Zackery, Mrs. Trowbridge, a battered Rance, and one uniformed officer. No doubt from the Sheriff's office.

She stumbled to a halt in front of them. They all stared and yelled, "There she is! Tava!" They rushed toward her. Aunt Kate got to her first. Tears of joy ran down her face. She threw her arms around Tava, and hugged her tightly. "Where have you been, Tava?"

Tava, panting from her race back, and trying to get her breath, said, "Give me a minute."

Dottie hugged her next, and pointed to the officer. "That's Sheriff Greene, and he's been searching for you. We all thought you'd been kidnapped!"

They all crowded around her, waiting for an explanation.

Shane stepped from Elisa's side and elbowed his way to Tava. He reached out his arms for her.

Tava, forgetting her jealousy of Elisa, collapsed into Shane's arms. She stared up through tears of relief.

"Don't talk until you're ready," Shane said in a gentle voice, and held her close.

Tava wiped the tears from her eyes. "I'm ready to tell you now."

CHAPTER TWENTY

Tava's thoughts were on Hobe's escape. She pulled gently away from Shane's embrace. She wiped the tears from her eyes.

"You won't believe where I've been!"

Everyone anxious to hear pressed around her, and said in unison, "Yes, we will!" "What happened? Were you kidnapped?" Dottie asked.

Over the din of voices Sheriff Greene introduced himself, and asked with an air of authority. "Do you need medical attention, young lady?"

Tava shook her head. "I'm good," she sputtered. She went through the whole story, telling about Hobe's actions and cowardice.

Sheriff Greene waved his hand for silence. "We already have an APB out for Hobe Yates for assaulting Rance Bottoms. He can't have gotten very far." He pointed toward Tava's car. We saw your car parked here, and found your tracks by the lake. We knew you had been there, but we didn't find your art paraphernalia. Right off we suspected you'd been kidnapped."

Aunt Kate piped up. "I reported to the Sheriff Rance had been beaten up and needed medical care."

The Sheriff waved his hand. "After questioning Rance, we suspected Hobe was responsible for your disappearance." He gestured toward Mr. Zackery. "Hobe's also a suspect in the theft of funds from Mr. Zackery's realty business."

Zack nodded in agreement, and pointed to Tava. "Young lady, I did not try to run you down. I loaned Hobe my car."

"I know now," she said, and noticed Rance looking battered and contrite. Rance hung back from the others. Then he pushed through to Tava: his head bowed, and whispered, "I have the tin box."

"Yes, I know," Tava said. "I sorry your great, great, grandmother was disinherited so long ago."

"Thank you," he said, but it's no reason for my being homeless. That is my own fault." He raised his voice and said to the group, "I admit my wrong doing, and I'm ready to face the consequences. You can arrest me now, Sheriff." He stuck out his hands to be handcuffed.

"Not so fast, Rance." The Sheriff shrugged. "It will be up to Tava to place charges against you."

"Before you get put in jail, Rance," Aunt Kate said, "You'd better see a doctor." "I believe you're right, Kate," Rance replied. "I think you've been punished already under the circumstances, Rance," Aunt Kate said. "But it's not up to me."

"We'll work something out, "Tava said, feeling no animosity toward Rance. Instead she felt compassion for his homelessness and his unfortunate circumstances.

"What was the Hobe's reason to beat you up Rance?" Dottie asked. Rance lowered his head, and spoke in a low voice. "I refused to do everything he had ordered me to do. He had promised I could continue to live here and work for him if I did everything he asked. I went along with him for a while, since I didn't have any other place to go. Whenever Hobe found out Tava was going to buy the old place, he became frustrated, and took it out on me. Said I hadn't done enough."

Mrs. Trowbridge spoke out. "What I'd like to know is what happened to Jess's furniture? He only gave me three pieces."

"I'd like to know that too," Dottie said.

"I can tell you," Rance volunteered.

"I helped Hobe move all those antique pieces from the old house in to my shed. I sure was cramped. I will help someone move the furniture back to the old house any time you're ready."

"Well. Isn't that something?" Mrs. Trowbridge said.

Tava gaped at the good fortune of finding the furniture.

Dottie clapped. "Thank goodness, I'll get to see the antiques whenever we get Cherohala restored"

Tava remembered Pepper, and turned to Aunt Kate. "Did Pepper come home?"

"Yes." A puzzled look crossed Aunt Kate's face.

"Good heavens! Now I understand what Pepper was trying to do! Lead me to the cliff! He kept acting strange; scratching to get out and whining to get back in. I was so upset when you didn't return, I couldn't think straight. Finally I put Pepper in the utility room and left him there."

Dottie edged close to Tava, "I talked to the loan officer at the bank. You'll have no trouble getting a loan for Cherohala. As soon as your dad gets here and signs on the dotted line, Cherohala will belong to you. I'll put up the funds for renovation, if I can be a partner in restoring the old mansion."

"You'll be my partner," Dottie," Tava gushed.

"Aunt Kate, you'll have to work with us as a consultant on the house and furnishing."

"Well, it will be something to keep me busy," Aunt Kate said.

"I'll need something to do, also," Mrs. Trowbridge said, nodding her head.

Tava imagined everything coming together like it should, until she glanced at Shane and Elisa.

They stood side by side, smiling, as if they shared a special secret. They turned and faced Tava.

"Tava," Elisa said, "I'm sorry we missed our lunch date. I had something important to tell you. Shane and I wanted you to be the first to know."

Tava's pulse raced, and her jealousy returned. She tried to steel herself for what she imagined Elisa was gong to say.

"Shane is my brother!" Elisa smiled.

"What!" Tava stared open-mouthed as the news sank in. "Really!"

Shane nodded. "When we found out we were both adopted, we compared our earlier experiences. When our memories sounded familiar to each other, we searched for evidence. At last we found proof."

"I'm so happy for you both!" Tava embraced them.

Everybody cheered.

THE SPELL OF CHEROHALA

CHAPTER TWENTY-ONE

The next morning Sheriff Greene phoned Tava the news of Hobe's capture and the recovery of the chest. She was needed at 2:00 o'clock in town at the municipal building to identify it. Aunt Kate, Dottie, Shane, Elisa, Mr. Zackery, Mrs. Trowbridge, and a few onlookers watched expectantly as Tava identified the chest.

Rance, looking lively, entered the room, and placed an opened rusty metal box in Tava's hands. Tava opened the box, and pulled out a yellowed parchment-like paper. On it was written the articles that were placed inside the chest.

Tava whispered to Rance, "When this is all settled, I want to talk to you about staying on as Cherohala's caretaker. Families should stick together."

Rance's face broke into a grin.

Tava looked at Dottie. "I think the first thing we should do is bring David's remains to the Henner cemetery to be interred with his family. They should be together."

"After all these years, its time," Aunt Kate said. "I wish we could right another wrong, and

Page 205 of 207

restore Rance's ancestor, Lavonia's inheritance."

"It seems Tava is doing the next best thing by letting Rance stay on as a caretaker of Cherohala," Dottie said.

The group clapped. A local photographer readied her camera as Tava stepped up and fingered the array of tarnished articles from the opened chest: a silver porringer, two silver candle holders, a candle snuffer, a silver belt buckle, an ivory inlaid jewelry box, a beaded necklace, a cameo brooch, and a handful of gold coins.

Aunt Kate spoke up. "At last Horace Henner's spirit can rest in peace. He hid the valuables in a good place."

"Tava, what are you going to do with all these items?" Sheriff Green asked.

"I'll return the chest and its contents to their proper place; the Cherohala Museum, Tava said, without hesitation.

"Right on!" Dottie said, and clapped.

Shane reached for Tava's hand, and squeezed it; his eyes twinkling. Tava beamed in happiness. With Shane by her side, and Cherohala to renovate, what more could she want?

ABOUT THE AUTHOR:

Joyce Rose Hensley Boyer grew up in Madisonville, in Monroe County, Tennessee. She attended and graduated from the University of Tennessee (UT), Knoxville, with a Bachelors Degree in Education. She met her husband of 50 years, Franklin Boyer, at UT.

She taught elementary school in Tennessee, North Carolina, and Virginia, and then retired to raise her two daughters with her husband, who was also a teacher for Henrico County, Virginia. She is a grandmother to three and great-grandmother to five.

Joyce has been writing for three decades and enjoys writing stories for young adults and children. Joyce has many other stories and books, which will soon be available for sale on Amazon.com and CreateSpace.com.

She is currently working on her memoirs relating funny and curious stories about her childhood with her siblings, cousins, and parents growing up in rural Madisonville, Tennessee during the depression and later years.

More of her short stories are available for free on the website: http://DawnDBoyer.com, which she shares with her story-writing daughter, Dawn D. Boyer. She welcomes her fans to write her at: JoyceHensleyBoyer@gmail.com.

15188962R00111

Made in the USA
Charleston, SC
21 October 2012